THE MIDAS CAT 3:

A Midas Cat in New York

TOMMY ELLIS

3 Spot Press

Praise for The Midas Cat series.

"Cleverly funny" - Louise Cannon, arts critic for Bookmarks and Stages.

"An absolute gem of a book" - Amazon review.

"Intelligent, zany. laugh-out-loud funny" - Amazon review.

"This is excellent" - Kaylee Gryba, author of Single and Catless.

"This was not only witty but funny, adventurous and well described" - Amazon review.

"A fantastic book that has it all" - J. Sheppard, author of Scottish Alliance.

"An excellent read" - Amazon review.

Copyright © 2020 Tommy Ellis

The right of Tommy Ellis to be identified as the author of the Work has been asserted by him in accordance to the Copyright, Designs and Patents Act 1988

All rights reserved. No part of this publication may be reproduced, stored in a retrieval system, or transmitted in any form or by any means without the prior written permission of the publisher, nor be otherwise circulated in any form other than that in which it is published and without a similar condition being imposed upon the subsequent purchase. All characters in this publication are fictitious and any resemblance to real persons living or dead is purely coincidental.

PUBLISHED BY
3 SPOT PRESS

ABOUT THE AUTHOR

Tommy has been a full-time musician and entertainer since 1988 and writes in clubland and holiday park dressing rooms whilst waiting for the bingo to finish. He is the author of The Midas Cat series of books and lives on a farm with his wife, three cats and chickens.

For Micheala

TOMMY ELLIS

Dogs have masters, cats have staff.

CHAPTER 1

Ralph

The first snow of the season had sprinkled New York with a light, almost dry dusting, and as Ralph stepped from the super-heated yellow cab onto the sidewalk, the hard cold almost punched his lungs out.

Still, it was nice to go Christmas shopping without having to check for the Biddles, the Falcon Hall loon squad, Frank Stone and his legalised gang of thugs, AKA The Flying Squad, Jeffrey the maniac doctor, or his cousin Rolph/Eric. They were either dead, declared criminally insane, were under investigation by Internal Affairs, or in jail for fraud. He'd been charged with murder and jumped bail. He'd then escaped to a secretive police state, been shrunk to the size of a microbe in order to spy on the West and hitched a lift home in the top pocket of the US president. Now he'd been declared innocent and sane and was also comfortably well off. So what did he care if his cousin was having a cosy Christmas sharing a cell with Britain's most notorious serial killer.

The only thing missing was his ex-wife Lauren. It would have been far better if she were by his side at this time of year, but what could he do? She'd left him because he hadn't provided her with the birthday present she really wanted – a legendary talking feline called a midas cat.

Macy's art deco storefront glittered with a million white stars that pierced the fading light. They really knew how to do Chrimbo in the States.

A live choir singing *Silent Night* amidst a thousand urgent shoppers seemed, at the very least, incongruous. A rousing chorus of *I Wish It Could Be Christmas Every Day* would have been a bit more like it, but nevertheless, it did put him in the right frame of mind to indulge in a spot of retail therapy.

Once his brain got used to the festive overload, he started checking the shop out properly, and what a shop. He could almost feel his arteries hardening by just looking at the cakes, marzipan and chocolates. Once he was finished in the food hall, he'd definitely have to book a liposuction session.

Leaning in to get a closer look at a gold leaf covered Christmas pudding, a nudge from an inconsiderate shopper almost launched him into the pudding pyramid. Spinning to face the clumsy tosser, he was about to rip out a tirade, when a glimpse of something horribly familiar stole his voice. Hopping through the grinding crowd was… 'The bloody midas cat.' The words came out as a whisper so faint, he wasn't actually sure if he'd said them out loud or not. How the hell could a talking cat in an *I heart New York* hoodie, Yankees baseball cap and pink handbag not get singled out as at least slightly odd?

A second jolt nearly catapulted him head-first into the neat arrangement. 'Oi, watch it!' The long face that looked back at him had a pair of felt ears nearly a foot long. One was standing straight up, whilst its partner had kinked in the middle, making it stick out to the side. The man's donkey mask now read 3 o'clock. Without a word, the masked moron shuffled back into the mob, and that's when Ralph spotted it. A huge donkey's head loomed out of the baubles and tinsel, and the sign above it read; *Donkeyman and Tabby McGill Ride Again!* He pushed through the throng to the merchandise stand. Racks of Donkeyman outfits stood alongside rows of tabby cat masks. No, the midas cat wasn't in New York. It was a kid in a mask. The latest in the franchise was due out on December 20th and *Silence of the Donkeys* was set to be a blockbuster.

The girl at the merchandise stand smiled at him hoping, no doubt, that he'd buy some of her crappy stuff. If she was on commission only, she'd already made a packet today. No, she was doing fine without him buying some Taiwanese injection moulded plastic. What he *was* after, though, was a new suit from the *You're Next* fashion house. *1920s gangster chic with a 21st century twist* was how it was advertised. Sharp suits with a modern cut in up-to-date fabrics and colours. *Al Capone would buy a You're Next suit* was what the TV advert said. A man standing on the running board of an old gangster-mobile would pass across the screen followed by a burst of machine-gun fire. Bullet holes would then appear under the *You're Next* logo.

He didn't usually buy into advertising shtick, but *You're Next* had really got his imagination going. That was the reason he was in New York in the first place. He didn't want to just pop to his local shopping centre, he wanted the full US experience. This was where prohibition took place, and this was where all the well-dressed mobsters plied their trade.

The suit was sharper than a Japanese chef's knife, and it even came with free entry into a competition. He had the chance to win a day being chauffeured in a stretched limo to the most exclusive restaurants and spend an evening at a Broadway showing of *Cats*. He could afford to do all that stuff anyway, but it would just feel good if he won it all, instead.

Now he had what he came for, it was time to eat. There was an Italian place in Greenwich Village that was supposed to be amazing.

He stepped out of the store into the frost-laden night pulling his new trilby further down onto his bald head, and just as he was about to hail a cab, the headline at a nearby newsstand grabbed his attention in both fists and refused to let go. CHICAGO MOBSTER, MICKEY EYEBALL, SUSPECTED OF PULLING THE TWIN-MING HEIST. Mobster? Heist? All that stuff was only some romanticised notion of a time long gone. Surely there wasn't really somebody called Mickey Eyeball?

The black limo idling at the kerb couldn't have been much shorter than twenty feet and must have arrived whilst his attention was on the newsstand. Some lucky bugger must have won the *You're Next* competition. They were in for a great night, but he didn't have time to stand about in refrigerated temperatures ruminating on someone else's good fortune.

He took a step forwards, intending to grab a taxi when the chauffeur, fully garbed in suit, tie and cap, walked around the front of the car, opened the rear door and ushered him in.

Ralph looked over his shoulder, expecting to see someone hurrying from the store into the leather upholstered wheeled palace. Nobody rushed forwards. He shrugged and continued walking.

The driver pointed at him. He looked around again just to make sure. No, there was nobody else, just him. Had he won the *You're Next* competition? His first night in The City That Never Sleeps, and he'd won, as the blurb said, *an evening of elegant dining and sophisticated entertainment.* Cool.

The chauffeur closed the door behind him with an overly heavy clunk, slid back into the driver's seat and pulled smoothly away from the kerb.

'This is fantastic.' Ralph leaned forwards in order to grab a few words. He'd won the contest, sure, but where were they going first? 'I was just wondering...' His sentence was cut dead as the glass privacy screen slid noiselessly up, isolating him from the driver. His mind was busily running along the *how rude* track when the sound of the central locking system trapping him in the back seat tripped the points, sending him down the *something's not right* line instead. 'Can we pull over for a sec?' The driver ignored him.

'Hello, can we stop for a minute? I need to get out.' He grabbed the door handle and pulled. Nothing. 'This isn't funny.' He banged his fist on the glass, and this time the chauffeur responded, and Ralph sincerely wished he hadn't.

The metallic click coming from the far side of the glass was made by the tip of the silencer that was screwed onto the end of the automatic pistol the man was holding.

CHAPTER 2

The Cat

New York was Cat's kind of town. They may not have had pubs, but they did have bars, clubs, hotels, restaurants and, of course, Broadway.

She'd been partying hard, and it was time for bed. The thought of hailing a cab, though, filled her with dread. Anyone's bum could have been on those seats. Urgh! A stretched limo, on the other hand; well, that was different. The man in the chauffeur's uniform and cap wasn't using it because he was too busy lurking in a doorway, smoking a cigarette. He wouldn't mind if she borrowed it for a few hours, would he? Once she'd finished with it, she'd leave it where he'd be able to find it, so no harm done.

Slipping in behind the wheel, she adjusted the seat and checked the ignition. He'd even left the keys for her. How considerate. She'd be back at her hotel in less than five minutes, and it was all due to the kind man in the chauffeur's cap.

When she drove away, though, he'd had the strangest reaction. The cigarette had fallen from his lips, and he'd sprinted after her shouting something about being a dead man. God knows what was wrong with him? He wasn't dead because dead men can't run and swear. Barmy!

The main thoroughfare was heavy with traffic, and she didn't fancy trying to park the behemoth on such a busy street. The last thing she wanted to do was scratch it after the owner had been so kind, so she pulled into an alley beside the hotel.

Cutting the engine, she reached for the door handle before pausing. That driver fellow had allowed her to borrow his lovely car for the evening. She couldn't possibly go without leaving him a thank-you note. The only problem, however, was not possessing anything to write either with or on. She thought for a moment. Whenever she went shopping, she put a pad and pencil in the glove compartment of whatever car she'd happen to borrow so she could do her list and tick off the stuff she'd bought. Why would anyone else do otherwise?

Apart from the service manual, the only thing in there was a wooden box about the length of a wine bottle and twice as wide. The nails securing the lid had been almost, but not entirely, removed. Was she about to leave it there without looking inside? Hell no. She was a cat. Nosiness was next to cattiness.

Packed in with wood shavings was a tatty old vase that had pictures of blue dragons and what looked like Chinese writing on it. It couldn't have been worth much. It wasn't as if it was new, or anything. Perhaps the man was taking it to the local dump? Well, she'd dispose of it for him. That was the least she could do to repay his kindness.

After thinking on it some more, she remembered her sister Yolanda; She liked old stuff. She was always going on about vintage this and antique that. Well, this vase was old. Perhaps she'd like it?

Teasing it from its box, she opened the clasp on her handbag and slid it inside. There wasn't room for much else, but that didn't matter.

Her second day had been even better than her first. What with sightseeing trips to the statue of liberty, the empire state building and Times Square, she'd even tasted her first genuine American hot dog with all the trimmings. Fantastic! The main reason she was here, though, was Adam Ant. A US tour, and her sister had bought her tickets for New York *and* LA. Unfortunately, it coincided with the professor's next children's lecture. Her last one had been a hoot. Especially the kid who'd been set light to. When he'd got his head almost blown off his shoulders, followed by a blasting with homemade gunpowder, though; well, that was priceless! It was such a shame she'd have to miss it.

Adam Ant, however, wasn't performing until tomorrow, so she had one more evening on the town, and a spot of shopping in the world-famous Macys was just the ticket. She couldn't use the limo, though, as the nice man who'd lent it to her had collected it. Either that or someone had nicked it. Maybe she shouldn't have left the keys on the passenger seat.

It was the second week of December, and the department store was in the Christmas fast-lane with its festive pedal mashed firmly into the cinnamon-scented floor mat.

The choir singing *Silent Night* would have been perfect if they hadn't been drowned out by the sheer number of shoppers, though. The only time Cat had ever seen that amount of people in one place was at an 80s reunion gig starring Boy George.

As she flowed through the sweat and perfume scented crowds towards the food hall, she glimpsed somebody who seemed almost, but not entirely, familiar. Some clumsy prat had barged into a bald man, nearly launching him head-first into a carefully constructed display of gold leaf covered Christmas puddings. She stared hard at the man as he spun to face the dexterously challenged moron and felt her recognition circuits crackle. It was that fantastic actor she'd seen back in September. During her local town's annual week-long carnival, he'd starred in a street theatre production and had even done his own stunts. He'd crashed a car, been shot at by undercover cops and even been held hostage by gun-toting tramps. Was it really him, though?

Deciding that the actor was, in actual fact, just another ordinary shopper, Cat shrugged and headed deeper into the store. It was time for some serious shopping, anyway.

The throng had been way too thick to make for a pleasant shopping experience. As amazing as Macys was, it was just too damned crowded. She needed an early night, anyway, if she was to be fresh for tomorrow's gig and headed out into the arctic evening.

A light dusting of snow had sparkled the city with a trillion diamonds, adding an extra layer of Christmasness to the spiced Big Apple. The only problem, however, was how different everything looked with an icing-sugar coating.

After walking for ten minutes, she couldn't be sure that she was even heading in the right direction. She was loathe to hail a cab, though, due to the proliferation of other people's backsides. No, if she kept on walking, she was bound to find her hotel sooner or later. It *was* the Waldorf Astoria, after all.

After another five minutes and a few minor detours, she accidentally found the hotel's rear entrance. It must have been the place. Well, it looked like the place. It was definitely posh enough. Once inside, though, the chemical tang of wet paint told her otherwise. Had she taken a wrong turn and ended up in another hotel?

The machine-gun clatter of a pneumatic drill was certainly something that hadn't been going on when she'd gone out. Maybe there was some sort of urgent work that needed to be done, like a burst water main, or something to do with gas? Whatever it was, she would just have to sleep with her earbuds in with Adam Ant playing on a loop.

The hazy view through the hanging plastic sheets confirmed her suspicions. Workmen were busy doing whatever it was workmen did. Deciding they'd probably be gone by morning, Cat pressed the elevator button.

The top floor wasn't as well-lit as she remembered, and she was sure there was a corridor when she was here last. Stepping out into what looked like an enormous living room, she fished in her handbag for her cigarettes and matches. With the vase in there, it was a bit of a squeeze, but so long as her fags and hip flask fit, it didn't matter.

Cigarette lit, she dropped the match onto a glass coffee table, only to watch it bounce twice and cartwheel onto the floor. She'd be in trouble if she burnt a hole in the carpet, but she'd lost sight of the still-glowing stick. Perhaps it rolled under the sofa. She shrugged and looked around the room. Laying on the white marble mantlepiece was a bundle of cigars tied together with wire. Maybe they were complimentary? Whether they were or not, Cat loved a good cigar.

She packed the hand rolled Cubans into the final few inches of space in her handbag and sniffed the air. A fireworky smell accompanied a funny fizzing sound. The non-stop drilling was bad enough, now kids were letting off roman candles nearby. Typical!

Sleep wasn't going to visit tonight, so it was time to put in a complaint to the manager in person.

She stuffed in her earbuds, selected Adam Ant's *Dog Eat Dog,* a good track to psych her up for an official complaint and stepped back into the elevator.

Glancing up at the arrow as it counted down dislodged an important memory. The Waldorf Astoria had more floors than were indicated. She *was* in the wrong building. She could be such an idiot at times.

The explosion that concluded the track on her iPod shook the elevator, flickering the lights. How was that even possible when the boom was only coming from her tiny little earbuds?

CHAPTER 3

Mickey Eyeball

Getting into The Harrington Building whilst renovation work was going on couldn't have been easier. A Hi-Viz jacket, hard hat and toolbelt, and he was not only in without having been questioned but was strolling around the Harrington's penthouse apartment unchallenged. Although *apartment* was a bit of an understatement. It occupied the entire top floor of the art deco highrise, was blingier than Elvis Presley's Jungle Room and deserted.

Donald Harrington was out of the country having evicted the entire building's-worth of tenants. He'd done it in order to *upscale* the tired interior and treble the rent, which was perfect. Noisy building work and no residents meant blowing the Harrington safe using his preferred method of TNT wouldn't attract any unwanted attention.

Don Vincenzo had told him to stop dynamiting

safes, especially after the disaster a few years back that had earned him his nickname. Having a glass eye really messed with his depth of perception, but that was a minor problem because he loved blowing shit up.

'Update your skills, Mickey. Move into the 21st century, Mickey. 'Yeah, well fuck you, Vince,' he muttered as he pulled the hammer head off of a stick of explosives. Dynamite disguised as tool handles was genius. Nobody worried about chisels or a claw hammer. This robbery was strictly off the books, though. Every job he did, he paid fifty percent to The Syndicate for their legal fund and insurance policy which consisted of paying off both state and federal police and the *handling* of a selection of judges. It wasn't making him rich, though, was it?

As he ran the old-school gunpowder-impregnated fuse across the floor, his mind snapped back to the previous job he'd been press-ganged into. A pair of Ming-dynasty vases from The Harrington Collection had been put on show in New York's Metropolitan Museum of Art. Virtually unfencable, and therefore practically worthless, he had been drafted onto the team for his explosives expertise. Vincenzo hadn't complained about updated skills when good old Mickey had got them in, had he?

All that work to lift some pottery that was being given away to the triads. Well, the bearer bonds in this safe would look after him in his old age. All one hundred percent of them.

'Fuck you, Vince,' he said again and grinned to

himself. If it hadn't been for The Twin-Ming heist, he wouldn't have thought of the Harrington safe and the near-deserted building in the first place. He was going to enjoy his retirement. He'd be able to live a stylish life and had already started with a new suit from the *You're Next* range he'd seen in Macys. So what if the guys took a rise out of him for dressing like a prohibition era mob boss. Dressing sharp makes you look sharp, think sharp and act sharp, and what was so wrong about that? He needed to be as sharp as possible if he was going to get away with this private mission.

He poked the fuse into the bundle of sticks. Once lit, he'd have fifteen seconds until boom time, then maybe two minutes to clear the safe of its valuable paperwork before a leisurely ride down in the elevator. He'd stagger from the lift, feigning shell-shock, yell for someone to call the fire department, and then he'd slip away in the confusion. The plan was nothing if not classy.

He put the spare bundle of TNT on the marble mantlepiece and froze. The elevator had just pinged. Nobody was meant to be up here. He was supposed to have had the whole penthouse to himself. Shit! Had he forgotten to disable the damned elevator controls? With no time left for anything else, he hit the wall switch, killing the power to the chandelier which plunged the apartment into not-quite total darkness.

The elevator was situated in the far wall, giving whoever was in it a panoramic view of the whole room. If he got caught up here with two bundles of dynamite, not only would he serve time, he'd serve time knowing Don Vincenzo knew he was doing an off-the-books job. That was something you just didn't do. Especially when The Syndicate owned most of the prison guards in county lock-up.

The dining room, bathroom and kitchen were too far away. He'd never make it in time. Meeting with an accident whilst in jail was a very real threat, though, so he had to quit flapping and start acting.

A steadily widening stream of light cut across the carpet as the elevator doors slid open. If he was going to do anything, he had to do it now.

The strongbox he'd come for was floor mounted and hidden under a panel in the walk-in wardrobe. It was a Halloween horror film cliché, but the alternatives were what, exactly?

He stepped inside and pulled the coats across. With no time left to close the doors behind him, he stared out into the room from between a heavy winter sheepskin and a lightweight raincoat. What he saw doubled his already dangerously high pulse rate.

The match that flared in the darkened room flashbulb-lit a face that was impossible. It looked like that superhero's sidekick, Tabby McGill. He'd seen the films and the crappy masks you could buy, but that was no mask.

He crossed himself and silently prayed to Jesus, Mary, and The Almighty Father. He knew it was useless, though, because he was staring at the legendary midas cat. If you saw it, you died. Just like a banshee, it foretold a death, and he knew it wasn't a fairy tale. He'd heard about some English Lord who'd seen it before getting run over by a car, a banker driven mad by it before it turned him into the un-dead, and a gang of loan sharks who were gunned down after seeing it. Now here he was looking into its demonic furry face.

The glowing match dropped from the cat's paw onto the coffee table. He couldn't be completely certain, but hadn't it bounced before hitting the carpet? Somewhere down there was the fuse. The odds of match and fuse lining up were size-of-the-galaxy large, but that didn't factor in supernatural intervention.

The silent prayer notched up in its urgency as the cat picked the spare bundle of dynamite from the mantlepiece. Holy Mary, Mother of God, the fucking cat was going to blow him up!

He scrunched his eyes shut. His ma had told him stories about the old country. Stories about leprechauns and fairies, about changelings and trolls. The most terrifying story, though, the story that made him wet the bed until he was five years of age, was the story about the midas cat. Up until a few years back he thought it was just a tall tale made up to control a wayward three-year-old Mickey.

'Eat up your porridge, Mickey.' Ma's soft Southern Irish lilt always had an edge hard enough to knock your teeth out when she spoke of the midas cat. 'If you don't, the midas cat will turn you into the cursed un-dead.'

When he'd turned twelve, he'd told her it was all make-believe crap and had paid with the fastest backhand he'd ever seen. Actually, that was the point. He hadn't seen it. He'd have ducked if he had.

'The more you disbelieve, the worse it will be when the talking cat comes for you.' That was what she'd said, and now he knew how right she'd been all along.

The fizzing that accompanied the odour of sulphurous burning chemicals was a sound and smell he knew well...too bloody well! Those treble-lottery-winning odds he was thinking about earlier had just dropped to zero. Indecision had poured superglue into his brain, preventing not only any coherent thought but any action likely to save his life. If he stayed in the closet with the dynamite, he'd die. If he ran into the room with the midas cat, he'd die. If he pulled out the fuse, the cat would hear him, and he'd die.

He peered out from between the coats. The evil spirit had put in a pair of earbuds. Earbuds? Evil spirits wear earbuds? Mickey knew his pop history and recognised the tinny rhythm that rose above the hissing of the fuse. Adam Ant's *Dog Eat Dog* was his final thought.

CHAPTER 4

Ralph

Trepidation had fled, leaving Ralph with pure uncooked fear. 'Let me out of here!' He banged on the courtesy screen once again. If this was part of the competition win, he wasn't impressed. It was one thing gearing up an advertising campaign around prohibition era gangsters, but an armed driver was beyond wrong.

The glass slid down, stopping when a gap of less than a centimetre had opened.

'Are you gonna shut the fuck up, or am I gonna have to make ya?'

The chauffeur was waving the gun around again. No, this was nothing to do with any competition. If it wasn't, then what the hell was it?

Ralph pulled on the door handle again, but of course it wouldn't open. He was being abducted. But why, and by whom? In a previous life he'd been a banker operating in the grey areas of hedge fund management, offshore tax havens and schemes that amounted to nothing short of money laundering. He'd dealt with people so shady, it was a wonder he ever managed to see their faces. Had he upset the wrong oligarch?

The big car had come to a stop, and Ralph looked around. Thankfully, they weren't in some garbage-strewn alleyway where, in the movies, victims were forced to kneel before being shot in the back of the head. They were idling at a set of traffic lights and right next to them was New York's finest. The cop in the cruiser had to have been a caricature, though. Double chinned and munching on a doughnut, Ralph wondered how he'd be any use in a chase on foot. Then he remembered. All US cops are armed. Bullets run faster than people.

'Hey, fat cop!' he yelled. 'Hey, help. I'm being kidnapped!' He beat his fist on the side window and waved his arms in a *help, I'm drowning* manner.

'He can't see you,' said the driver before cranking the sound system. Italian opera flooded the car with sensual overload. Under normal conditions he would have sat back and let the music flow into him, allowing it to take him on its journey of classical ecstasy, but he'd been abducted.

He banged on the limo-tinted glass for a final time as the police car turned right at the junction. He couldn't be seen; he couldn't be heard. He was in the back of what he could only assume was a mafia staff car and not, as he originally thought, a fashion house rental, and he was on his way to his own execution.

As the car glided through the city, Ralph tried to figure out two things. Who wanted him dead and how could he escape? Was this something to do with Lauren's father? That old bastard had never liked him. It couldn't be the Biddles. They were either dead or locked away indefinitely, and as for his useless cousin, he was, well, useless.

His mind pulled on strings that led nowhere. Did this have something to do with the headline he'd seen earlier? The Twin-Ming heist, that was it. He quickly put that idea back in its box. He wasn't a gang member and didn't have anything to do with any heist. Regardless of any of that, though, he *was* being taken somewhere by an armed thug.

That fact alone meant that he needed to get out. Not just out of the car, but out of New York, out of America. He had to run. As soon as he could, he'd make a break for it. It was his only chance. OK, he only had one real foot, but as he found out when those psychotic loan sharks were after him, adrenaline gives you, if not superhuman strength, maybe that extra burst when you really needed it.

The limo had pulled off the main thoroughfare into an alley just as Ralph had predicted. This was it. Escape or die.

CHAPTER 5

Don Vincenzo

Don Vincenzo bit down on the vaper. It wasn't a Cuban cigar, but his doctor had warned him to stop smoking or risk a coronary. It wasn't smoking that was going to stop his heart today, though, was it? Oh no. One of the Twin Mings that was lined up to prevent a war with the triads had been stolen.

'Jesus Christ!' he blurted out before looking at the hotel suite's ceiling. 'Sorry, Lord,' he muttered before crossing himself.

His driver, Pauly, had just given him the news. Some scumbag had had the audacity to lift a vase that he'd gone to the effort of stealing, and the worst part of this debacle was that only a handful of people knew about it. The people that knew where that fuck-ugly lump of china was were *his* people. They were made guys. Made guys didn't pull that kind of shit.

'Jesus fucking Christ!' He looked up again. 'Yeah, Lord. I know. I'm sorry. I'll make it up to ya.' What the hell was going on? Was someone making a move on him? It wouldn't be the first time.

He stopped pacing. He hadn't even realised he'd started until his belly was pressed up against the door. He'd had Pauly put the vase in the glovebox of the limo because it was so obvious, nobody would think to look there. Pauly knew, but if he'd stolen it, he wouldn't fess up about it going missing, would he? No, but what about that myopic Irish prick Mickey Eyeball? The shifty bald fuck had a habit of disappearing when he was supposed to be on a job and reappearing a couple of days later flush. The psychotic cyclops was doing private jobs. He was certain of it. Only, he couldn't prove it. Yeah, well, when he shows up this time, he'll wish he hadn't.

He puffed out a cloud of lemon scented steam and frowned. Lemon? Whoever heard of lemon smokes? Quit smoking, go on a diet, cut down on the booze. Was life even *worth* living? His pa had dropped aged forty, though, and if he wanted a long life, the doc had strongly advised he lived a healthy one. A long miserable fun-free existence. If that wasn't bad enough, he had the Chinese to deal with, and that was all Mickey's fault. He wouldn't be surprised if the damned firebug had a self-published book out. *Children's Crafting Fun With C4.* The idiot had blown up a triad soldier by accident during a co-opted bank raid and swore the midas cat did it. The moron was still alive, wasn't he? Legend said that if you saw it, you either died, or joined the rapidly swelling army of the un-dead.

He needed Mickey to straighten this mess out, but there was a lack of anything remotely Mickey-shaped. The vase had vanished. Mickey had vanished. Einstein wouldn't have pondered over-long with that problem, would he?

His guts gurgled. Living on lettuce and muesli couldn't possibly be doing him any good. Rabbit's breakfast and shredded cardboard? That wasn't food.

He hustled to the bathroom and stared into the mirror as his innards fought a civil war amongst themselves. The top of his hairpiece stared back, and he wondered why every bathroom mirror in every hotel was mounted too high. Then his mind snapped back to the imminent gang war that had every chance of erupting in the next few hours.

The Chinese were expecting delivery of both vases. Today. If he showed up with just the one, Mr Xao would consider it an insult. The second vase and Mickey had to be found. Find one, find the other, and somebody had to know something. That was why an extraordinary meeting had been set up in the Waldorf Astoria's main conference suite. One of his made guys knew something, and he fully intended to get the info out of him. Even if that meant wasting some of them. Shit, he hadn't killed anyone since 1997. His priest wasn't going to be happy with him, but this was an extreme problem that needed an extreme remedy.

CHAPTER 6

The Cat

It had been too cold to walk and besides, she'd got lost. Admitting defeat, she'd hailed a cab, and as soon as she'd stepped inside, her sensitive olfactory system had suffered. Perfume both cheap and expensive had fought against sweat, farts and various other unmentionable odours, and there was a crunchy feel underfoot that she just didn't want to think about.

Still, she was back at her hotel now, her cab ride a, thankfully, fading memory.

The snow had started falling properly outside. Not that timid, tiny-flaked stuff, but the full-bodied blizzard material that would bring the UK to a paralyzed stand still in under an hour, so she was glad to be inside where it was not only warm, but where it had a bar. The lift pinged and the doors slid open. She smiled at the thought of a couple of Manhattans as she stepped out onto the third floor and swung her handbag in a happy arc. She'd pop to her room, freshen up and head back downstairs to join the chic in-crowd.

The dull thud rudely interrupted her reverie as her bag hit the vase of flowers. As quick as Cat's reactions were, they weren't quick enough to stop it tumbling from the small table.

Water glugged out, soaking the carpet. The corridor was empty, so nobody had seen anything, but unfortunately the vase had a crack running from the lip to the base. If she put it back, someone would spot the damage, and she'd be in a heap of American-style trouble. That would probably mean a trip downtown in the back seat of a police cruiser and hours of questioning in a room with a large two-way mirror on the wall. At least, that was what happened on TV. Luckily, she had the solution to her problem nestling in her handbag. If she swapped the old piece of junk she'd found in the limo for the busted piece of new junk, nobody would know the difference. Who really took that much notice of bits of crockery, anyway?

She slipped the Chinese-looking vase out of her bag, arranged the flowers in it and stuffed the broken one into a nearby litter bin. By the time anyone noticed, she'd be back in her room examining the contents of the mini bar.

As she made her way to her room, she noticed an *Alice in Wonderland* sized door. It was more like a square hole in the wall because there wasn't actually a door there at all. A metal toolbox sat to one side of it along with half a dozen brass screws. Cat's curiosity gene overrode any safety concerns she may have had, and she stepped towards it, poking her head inside.

A square, badly lit, metal corridor stretched off into the distance and warm dry air wafted from it. Whatever that thing was, she had to... no, she *needed* to investigate. Whatever it was and wherever it led, she had an urge to find out more.

After a minute of walking, the feeble light faded to a thick darkness that even Cat had problems seeing through. She'd gone too far to go back and besides, if she backed out now, she'd never find out what the secret corridor was all about. What she needed was a little exploring music. Fishing in her pelt, she dug out her iPod, stuffed in her earbuds and cranked the volume.

After another minute or so, an electric-light glow from up ahead started pushing back the darkness. She must have been nearing the end of the passage. The hotel was built during the prohibition era. That much she knew. The corridor could be a disused booze-smuggling route. Cool!

She'd reached a T-junction. The left passage led away into darkness, whilst the right-hand turn ended at an art deco grille. That was where the light was coming from. As she stared at the grate, she realised what it was. This was no secret tunnel; it was a hot air heating duct that some worker-type person had left the grille off of. What was she going to do now, though? She could go back, but that was too far. Alternatively, she could charge the grille, breaking out into the room beyond. Yes, That was a plan.

Adam Ant's Stand and Deliver had hit its chorus and she howled along as she accelerated towards the heating vent.

CHAPTER 7

Ralph

Fat white flakes swirled in the eddies of steam puffing from wall vents, but the snow was too powerful to be beaten by a few breaths of heated vapour. The alleyway was just big enough for the limo to squeeze into with space for the doors to open either side. Any narrower, and the car would have become a prison... or a tomb.

Ralph looked out of the rear window. It hadn't been entirely whited out yet, but it wouldn't be long. The alley's entrance was only ten, or so, metres away, but it might just as well have been a thousand. What with the snow, and his false foot, Ralph didn't like the odds of not face-planting within the first couple of steps. That didn't mean he wasn't going to run, though.

The chauffeur stepped out of the car and tapped on the side window with the gun's muzzle. This was it. Run or paint the snow red.

The central locking was too loud and the snow too bright. When his real foot hit the soft top layer, he felt it give way to the crunch of the frozen powder beneath. The adrenaline dump was so violent, it caused an uncontrollable shake. He clenched his fists to hide the tremor and eyed the alley's mouth. People rushed in and out of taxis and traffic clogged the city street. He could see them, but they couldn't see him. Couldn't or wouldn't. It was like seeing someone getting beaten up. Don't get involved, don't get drawn in. The bad guy might turn on you instead. No, nobody was coming to help.

He pushed off with his right foot, shoving the armed driver aside as he did so. If his prosthetic left foot behaved itself, he might just live to see the morning.

As he hit the compressed tyre track, his leg squirrelled out from under him just as an unmistakable *phut* sounded from behind. He'd never heard a real silenced gun being fired, but he'd seen enough movies to give him a pretty good idea of how one sounded.

As he slammed into the deepening snow, a zinging whirr buzzed past his head.

'Get up, ya fucking prick!' The chauffeur grabbed his arm and hauled him to his feet. This was looking more like an Al Pacino gangster movie every second. Ralph's mind spun as he tried to figure out what was going on. He'd obviously pissed someone off to the extent of extreme violence. Who though? Drug dealer? Worse? What was worse than a pissed off drug dealer? The mafia? Oh, Jesus no. Not the mafia.

'Come on, ya shitstick. Move! The boss wants to see ya.'

'OK, OK.' Ralph spat out the mouthful of dirty snow he'd nearly swallowed in his fall.

'Hey,' said the chauffeur as he prodded Ralph in the back with his pistol. 'What's with the stupid fake limey accent? Speak properly, for crying out loud!'

The accent he was using was the only one he had, so why he'd been accused of putting it on was a bit more than odd.

The hum of the main street faded the further up the alley they went. At least he hadn't been executed. Well, not yet anyway.

'Knock twice on the door,' said his captor.

Tucked away between two industrial sized wheelie bins was a grubby grey door with no visible handle. Ralph rapped on it as instructed, and it was immediately opened by a man who couldn't have been much wider than a broom handle. A hairnet covered an unruly mop of greasy tangles, and a pair of dead flint-chip eyes stared out of a face so devoid of colour, it was almost pale green.

'You got him,' he said in a flat monotone. 'Conference room. Third floor. All the made guys are already there.'

After his speedy tour of the kitchens, Ralph was hustled through the restaurant into the main body of the hotel. The art deco opulence was unmistakable. He was in The Waldorf Astoria. On a normal day, he would have booked a table, or maybe just had a drink at the bar. But today wasn't normal. The clues were all there; the coded knock, the mention of *made guys,* and even the world's most dangerous washer-upper. Tonight he had an appointment with the New York cosa nostra.

After a terrifying gun-point ride in the elevator, they arrived on the third floor and marched down a deserted corridor. The door they stopped at had a side table to the left of it with a small Chinese-looking vase filled with lilies that wafted a funereal scent. Ralph knew whose funeral they were going to be used for.

'In ya go.' The chauffeur pushed Ralph towards the room. He took a squelching step forwards. Someone had spilled a jugful of water right by the door. Was the handle wired to the mains? With the puddle earthing him, he'd die instantly. He dismissed the thought as ludicrous. The mafia didn't do stuff like that, they shot you in the back of the head. He touched the handle with a fingertip expecting a lightning crackle anyway. Nothing. Well, he had to be sure.

The room was every bit as luxurious as he thought it would be. The wood panelling gave it an air of Edwardian smoking room, but the dragstrip length dark oak table was all business. There had to have been twenty chairs around it and sitting dead centre was a Chinese looking vase that was more than slightly familiar. He'd have easily placed it if he wasn't put off by the six serious-looking, sharp-suited men staring at him.

Without a word, one of the men threw a newspaper down onto the table. Ralph was drawn to the familiar headline: CHICAGO MOBSTER, MICKEY EYEBALL, SUSPECTED OF PULLING THE TWIN-MING HEIST. With the paper fully open, though, he could see the photo under the writing. Staring back at him and wearing an identical suit was, well... him. Standing outside a 1930s skyscraper was either a long lost twin he never knew he had, a clone, or himself.

The picture had, apparently, been taken yesterday outside the Harrington Building.

'Well?' The man who'd dropped the newspaper stepped towards him.

Well what? Ralph's mind tried unsuccessfully to piece together the impossible puzzle. If the picture was taken yesterday, and he hadn't bought the suit until today, he either had a doppelganger, or somebody owned a genuine working time machine. Either way, it couldn't mean anything good.

CHAPTER 8

Don Vincenzo

Don Vincenzo stopped outside the conference suite and farted. All that so-called healthy food he had to eat messed with his innards. Wind, heartburn, irritability. Christ, what he wouldn't give for a twelve-inch meat feast pizza washed down with a quality red wine.

'You OK, Boss?'

Vincenzo looked up at his personal bodyguard who always reminded him of Lurch from that old TV show, The Addams Family. 'Seriously, Al?' He shook his head. 'I spent most of the morning on the can, I'm trying to head off a gang war, and one of my made guys has stolen one of the Mings.'

'Sorry, Boss.'

Vincenzo reached for the suite's door handle, his foot squelching on the puddled carpet. 'What now?' He looked down. He'd just had his shoes polished to a near mirror shine, and now splats of dirty water speckled their once-perfect sheen. 'Why do they bother paying the damned staff if they can't even clear up a simple spill?'

'I don't know, Boss.'

'I didn't mean... oh, never mind.' Al was as loyal as a highly trained gun dog and twice as lethal, but everyday nous was an ingredient that God had left out of the mix.

The only sound in the conference suite was the warm air breathing from the grate high on the wall. His made guys looked on wordlessly as he pulled out his nine millimetre and screwed in the silencer. That act alone usually had, what he liked to call, the *squeal effect.* If anybody knew anything, they'd normally blab about now.

He looked from face to face. What he saw was obedience, respect and, in a few cases, love. All except Mickey. The one-eyed shit looked as though he'd loaded his pants and was trying to get comfortable. That look was either fear, guilt, or an unhealthy mix of the two. Oh yes, Mickey was guilty all right. Vincenzo nodded slowly, marshalling his thoughts. Stealing the peace offering that was supposed to smooth away the myopic idiot's own fuck up was just the kind of stupid-ass thing he'd do. He couldn't have done it alone, though. Someone else had to have been involved, but who?

'Mickey, Mickey, Mickey.' Vincenzo reached up and rested a hand on the man's quivering shoulder. 'What am I going to do, eh?' He kept his voice light.

Decades of experience told him he got better results that way. 'The triads are in the building, Mickey.' He patted the shoulder. 'They're expecting delivery of the Twin-Mings. The *Twin* Mings. If Mr Xao doesn't receive the Twin-Mings in...' Vincenzo pulled his sleeve back and tapped his watch. '...less than an hour, he ain't gonna be happy. If he ain't happy, I ain't happy.'

Vincenzo readjusted his stance, settling his gut over his belt, which released at least a pint of trapped wind. Goddammit! How was he supposed to come across as a menacing mob boss if he couldn't stop farting?

Barely controlled snorts of laughter evaporated when Vincenzo shot his *mafioso-death-stare* at the assembled group. Hilarity had its place, but not in a serious meeting. At least they had the sense to can the giggles, though. That meant he wouldn't have to maim any of them. Well, not yet, at any rate. If none of them grassed or owned up to helping Mickey, that would soon change.

'You've been careless, Mickey.' He prodded the man in the stomach with the tip of his pistol. 'Not only have you got yourself onto the front page, you've betrayed my trust.'

'I'm not Mickey.'

Vincenzo's thought-train de-railed. Was the moron talking in a limey accent, or had he imagined it? 'Say that again... slowly.'

'I'm n-not Mickey.'

What the hell was he playing at? It was one thing

putting on a fake accent to fool the cops, but he was amongst colleagues. He was part of the circle of trust. Trust? The one-eyed idiot had stolen one of the Mings and was now talking like an extra from a Guy Ritchie movie. Vincenzo's patience ran out of road. 'Speak properly, ya stupid shit-heel!' He slammed the gun into the side of the other man's head, popping out his glass eye. It hit the table, bouncing twice before rolling onto the floor.

'Pick that up, ya fucking firebug, and stop talking in that ridiculous accent!'

Whilst Mickey scrambled about on the floor, Vincenzo's thought-train chugged back to life. He had to find out who else was involved, because it could be a full-blown take-over bid. He needed to focus the men's minds, and the best way to do that was to sweat them. Sweat them fast.

'OK, here's what we're gonna do.'

A loud clonk came from under one of the chairs, and Mickey reappeared holding his glass eye. Jeez, he should have let that one go years ago. Was he getting too soft?

'Five minutes. That's how long you've got to tell me who else was involved. You either tell me, or I start shooting your toes off.' He turned towards the door, pulled it open, farted once again and stepped through it, closing it behind him. This time nobody giggled.

CHAPTER 9

Ralph

Ralph stared from the newspaper to the serious-looking men and back to the newspaper again. Wrong place, wrong time sounded like a cliché, but it wasn't. It was real. If he hadn't been in New York buying a stupid gangster suit in the first place, he wouldn't be in a room with half a dozen genuine gangsters.

The hoodlum snatched up the paper, rolled it up and used it to point at the vase on the table.

'Where's the other one, Mickey?'

Ralph's mind clicked in another of the mental jigsaw pieces. The design on the vase was definitely Chinese. Was it one of the Twin Mings? Before he had a chance to speak, the door swung open, and the six men straightened up in an almost military fashion.

The first man to enter would have been the perfect body double for Boris Karloff's monster in the classic Frankenstein movies. The second man, however, resembled a slightly chubbier version of Danny DeVito. Ralph conceded that *chubby* was a bit of an understatement. If the man was three feet taller, he'd have been a bit fat. This fellow was almost perfectly round but had an aura that demanded respect.

The be-wigged beachball reached into his inside pocket and, without a word, screwed a silencer onto the barrel of an automatic pistol. He then looked at every man, holding each gaze for a brief moment. When he got to Ralph, his eyes narrowed, and he nodded. Narrowed eyes and a nod couldn't have meant anything good.

'Mickey, Mickey, Mickey.' When the man reached up and rested a hand on Ralph's shoulder, he felt like screaming.

'What am I going to do, eh?' The mini mob boss was talking in a light sing-song voice, but Ralph could almost feel the murderous intent flowing from his fingertips.

'The triads are in the building, Mickey.'

The triads? He shouldn't have been surprised, though. The rule says that if you think things are as bad as they can get, that's when they get a whole lot worse.

The man patted his shoulder. 'They're expecting delivery of The Twin-Mings. The *Twin* Mings.' He drove home the word *twin* with the fervour of an over-excited preacher.

'If Mr Xao doesn't receive The Twin-Mings in…'

The micro-mobster pulled back the sleeve of his obviously handmade pinstripe with theatrical over acting. '...less than an hour, he ain't gonna be happy. If he ain't happy, I ain't happy.'

If he ain't happy, I ain't happy? Even the white fog of fear couldn't prevent that last statement from lighting up the gang-speak-cliché alert. Did this bloke go to mafia school, or something?

The boss hefted his gut over his belt, releasing a long rumbling fart, and splutters of suppressed giggles came from some of the men. Laughing? At a mafia boss? Were they mad? The laser stare the little man shot at the assembled crowd killed any remaining good humour, and then he turned his attention back to Ralph.

'You've been careless, Mickey.' The prod from the small man's pistol made Ralph jump, even though he knew it was coming.

'Not only have you got yourself onto the front page, you've betrayed my trust.'

Being accused of betraying a mafia boss's trust was as good a death sentence as murdering someone in Florida. He wasn't Mickey Eyeball, though. He had nothing to do with any of this. Hell, he wasn't even American. That chauffeur didn't believe he was English, but surely somebody would realise. He had to straighten this out before he was entombed in concrete.

'I'm not Mickey.' Ralph could almost see the other man's thought computer run a diagnostic check.

'Say that again,' said the man, 'slowly.'

This was his only chance. If he wanted to live, he had to convince the psychotic midget that he wasn't Mickey Eyeball.

'I'm n-not Mickey.'

Mafia man's expression flicked through surprise and distrust before settling on anger.

'Speak properly, ya stupid shit-heel!' he yelled in his broad New York accent before hauling back with his gun hand and striking Ralph's temple.

Ralph had never been pistol-whipped before, and he hoped he'd never have to go through it again. Pain erupted in his head, sending sparks dancing across his vision, and the sudden draught in his empty socket meant he'd lost his glass eye as well.

'Pick that up, ya fucking firebug, and stop talking in that ridiculous accent!'

His only plan had failed. All he had to do was talk normally, but even that didn't work. With his head still jangling, he dropped to his hands and knees. He had to figure a way out of this. The only problem was not being a gangster. They were experienced killers, and he was an ex-banker. Selling this lot PPI insurance wasn't going to do him any good.

Grabbing his fake eye, he scrambled backwards from under the table just as the boss started talking again.

'OK, here's what we're gonna do.'

What they were going to do would probably involve more pain and a slow lingering death. He straightened up, his head connecting with the underside of a chair with a loud thunk.

'Five minutes,' said the boss. 'That's how long you've got to tell me who else was involved. You either tell me, or I start shooting your toes off.' He was addressing the whole room, but Ralph knew who the speech was aimed at. Well, at least he was right about the pain part.

The boss faced the door, opened it, farted once more and exited, followed by his horror movie bodyguard.

The second the door clicked shut, the shouting began. Who knew what? Was it Pauly the chauffeur? Was it even a made guy? Mickey wasn't acting alone, so who was helping him?

Fingers pointed and chests were prodded as the volume level rose.

Throughout the increasingly heated argument, everybody seemed to have forgotten about the chief suspect, Mickey, AKA Ralph. If they continued to fight amongst themselves, maybe they'd ignore him completely. That's when plan B landed in his head fully formed. If he slipped out of the door, he could hide in the toilets until everything had calmed down and catch an earlier flight back to the UK.

He edged towards the door, heartrate pushing blown-vessel levels. Two more steps and he'd be out of there. He reached for the handle, fingers just touching the cold brass. Without daring to look back, he gripped the lever. Turn, open, slide out, then run for the stairs like his arse was on fire.

He froze when a single voice cut through the

racket, silencing the hubbub.

'Hey, Mickey! Where the fuck do you think you're going?'

His throbbing headache evaporated as bile filled his mouth with its bitterness. He wasn't going anywhere.

Hands gripped his lapels and tore him away from the exit and freedom.

'This shit's all your fault, Mickey!' They crowded around him, faces twisted with a brand of anger reserved for discovered adulterers, traitors and dog owners who allow their pets to crap under the kiddy swings.

'Where's the vase, Mickey? Where's the…?' The moustachioed man who had hold of him was shushed by an acne-scarred gangster with slick black hair so obviously dyed, it looked blue.

'Tony,' said the man holding Ralph. 'This better be important.'

'Yeah, yeah,' said Tony. 'It is. Listen.' He waved his hands, signalling for silence.

Above the background breathing of the hot air central heating, a cat's meow accompanied a faint bass note and terrifyingly familiar rhythm, that, if heard in isolation wouldn't have meant much. Heard together, though; well, that was an omen of revelatory proportions.

'Hey,' said Tony. 'A little pussycat's trapped in the heating duct.' He dragged a chair over to the wall, stepped up and, with the blade of his flick-knife, prised the heating vent open with a screech.

Ralph felt sick. Adam Ant's *Stand and Deliver* was getting louder, as was the off-key howling. He hadn't been mistaken in Macys. It wasn't a kid in a mask. Oh, Jesus. They were all going to die.

'The midas cat! Satan's pet is going to kill us all! Run!' Ripping free of the gangster's grip, Ralph took a step towards the doorway, only to find it blocked by a man wearing Buddy Holly specs.

CHAPTER 10

The Cat

Adam Ant's dandy highwayman pushed Cat to maximum acceleration. If she was going to bust through the heating vent, she needed to pour all her energy into hitting her top speed.

As she neared the grille, a face appeared on the other side of it. Even though the man was backlit, she could still make out the slicked back hair and acne scars. She was hustling towards the vent and the bloke's face at full throttle and was going so fast she'd never stop in time.

The man reached up, light glinting off his knife. Oh, God! Was he going to stab her? If she hit the brakes now, she'd slide on the metal ducting and straight onto the knife. There was only one thing for it. She'd have to go faster, attack being the best form of defence.

The screech of the vent being wrenched off the

wall was so loud, it could be heard over her iPod and singing. Now the vent had been removed, she had a clear view of the man, and he was making kissy faces at her. Kissy faces? He had a bloody flick-knife.

Reaching deep inside herself, she pulled out another one mile per hour. The end of the duct felt sharp through her ballet slippers as she launched herself into the room beyond.

Legs still pumping, she soared over the heads of the group of shocked-looking men, one of whom still had the heating vent in his hands.

The room was as tastefully furnished as anywhere else in the hotel, but from her vantage point of just below the ceiling, she could see it was some sort of meeting room. The table below her looked like an airport landing strip without the white lines but with an old vase, not control tower, sitting dead centre. She could have been mistaken, but wasn't it an exact replica of the one she had earlier? It could even be the same one. Maybe it had been moved by a member of staff. None of that mattered though, because the lump of pottery was in her flight path. That's when Cat's inner pilot kicked in: Disengage autopilot and prepare for manual landing. Notify air traffic control. *Mayday, mayday, request permission for emergency landing, over.*

ATC to Charlie Alpha Tango. Permission granted, over.

Roger that ATC. Over and out.

Maintain rate of descent, flaps up. Checking landing gear.

Cat touched down smoothly, and the men's faces blurred as she slid on the highly polished surface, vase looming large. With no chance of steering clear of the obstacle, she scrunched her eyes shut and braced for impact.

Stand and Deliver finished at the exact moment she made contact. The vase exploded with a loud pop as she shot through it, the shattered pieces whirring and zinging around the room before pinging and plunking off of light fixtures and wooden panelling. It was just as well the staff had put an old vase on the table. If it had been a new one, it would have been worth a lot more money.

Opening her eyes again to make sure she hadn't overshot the runway, she spotted a familiar face. Pinned against the door by a man in thick plastic glasses was the bald actor from that fantastic street theatre she saw in September. When she'd seen him in Macys earlier, she'd dismissed him as a lookalike, but now she was that much closer, she could see that it was definitely the same bloke. What was his name again? Her brain flicked through its inner rolodex: Raymond, Rob, Rolf, Ralph. That was it! Ralph! That meant that what she was witnessing was a play. The problem, however, was that plays were performed somewhere in public where people could see them. This was a private room, and the door was shut. That either made it a rehearsal or... Or what? If it wasn't a rehearsal, then that made it a not-rehearsal, which in turn made it real.

The suited men reminded her of a mafia film she'd

seen a while ago. If this was a not-rehearsal for a non-existent crime movie, she was in a roomful of gangsters.

Cat had run out of table and was still sliding at full speed. That left only one option. Engaging jump-jet propulsion, she sprung from the table's far edge but couldn't gain enough altitude to clear glasses-man's head. She was about to use a probably-armed criminal as a springboard. Well, at least that would give Ralph a chance to escape.

Time went into freeze-frame mode as she hit the back of the man's head, her legs concertinaing.

Ralph's expression had gone from terror, through surprise and had fixed on hope as glasses-man shot forwards. He headbutted the door with a splintering bish just as Ralph ducked.

The glasses the gangster was wearing had shattered and blood sprayed the wall as he slid, face first, down the door.

'The fucking midas cat!' yelled a man with a 1930s film star moustache. 'The bastard thing's real!'

Ralph was in trouble. She was in trouble. If she didn't save herself, she'd never be able to save Ralph.

'Jesus, Mary, and all the rest!' shouted acne-man. 'It ain't superstition!'

Cat leapt onto moustache-man's shoulder just as the knife left acne-man's hand. Cat anticipated the move and bounded up onto the chandelier.

The force of the throw sunk the blade up to the hilt into moustache-man's shoulder. The expected scream didn't materialise, though. Instead, he looked at the mother of pearl handle, reached for it with his right hand, slowly pulled it out and threw it back at acne-man.

An arc of blood flew from the whirling blade, pattering the ceiling and floor with a Jackson Pollack abstract, before pinning acne-man's hand to the wall.

'That's how to throw a knife, motherfucker!' He grunted in obvious pain as he lunged for the incapacitated acne-man. If this played out as she hoped it would, all focus would be on the two bloodied men. That would give her the opportunity to save Ralph *and* herself.

If you're going to hide in a wood, climb a tree. It's simple but effective because looking up is too much of an effort. From her perch on the light fitting, she watched as the other three men crowded around the upcoming fight. They'd forgotten about her and forgotten about Ralph. They all had their backs to her apart from acne-man, and he was a bit pre-occupied with trying not to die.

She scanned the room. Where had Ralph gone? Once the fight was over, she and him would become the centre of attention once again, so she had to act fast.

He hadn't gone out of the door, and there was nowhere in the room to hide... unless... She jumped to the thick carpet as quietly as she could and dropped into a crouch. There he was. He was peering out from under the table, his face a shade above Dracula-grey.

The fight had gone from name calling to actual physical pain. It sounded as though moustache-man was twisting the blade as acne-man's swearing liquified into high intensity screaming. He wouldn't be able to take much more of that sort of treatment and would probably faint. Then everyone else would get bored and remember her and Ralph.

She beckoned to the terrified actor who shook his head. She knew acting when she saw it, and this wasn't it. She had to coax him out, or if that didn't work, drag him out.

The shouts and taunts from the far side of the room were dying down. They had to go. Reaching a paw under the table, she grabbed Ralph's hand. It was icy cold in spite of the central heating and slick with sweat. That meant she'd have to hold on tight.

She took up the slack and hauled on the dead weight. If he didn't do something to help himself, he was going to be as blood smeared as the gangsters with a severe lack of life to add to his troubles.

As Cat pulled once again, Ralph finally got the message and scrambled out from under the table.

She pointed to the uncovered heating duct, hopped onto the chair acne-man had moved earlier and sprang into the aluminium tunnel.

After three steps into the darkness, she stopped. What was taking Ralph? If he spent any more time in that room, he'd be the next one with perforations. The fight was winding down. As soon as one of the men turned around... Cat didn't want to think about it. She crept back to the room hoping he was still alive.

CHAPTER 11

Ralph

Tiny fragments of pottery clattered and pinged off the furniture, but the cat just kept sliding. It was lined up perfectly with the thug who had him pinned to the door. Oh, Jesus, the bloody creature was about to slam into his captor. The gangster wasn't paying any attention to the carnage unfolding around him, though. It was as if a mythical talking cat hadn't just appeared from a hot air duct. He was staring at Ralph through his chunky glasses with high intensity hate and was obviously blanking everything else out. This bloke had probably killed before, and once the flying furball from hell messed up his dodgy hairdo, he was going to release the safety catch.

From over Buddy Holly's shoulder, Ralph watched the animal spring from the table's edge with the grace of an ice dancer and alter position in mid-flight. Whatever he thought of the midas cat, he had to admit that it had the moves. It had lined itself up with the back of Buddy's head, and as soon as the ballet slippers connected, the thug's expression went from kill-mode to what-the-fuck mode in less than half a second.

Ralph's thought process accelerated. He knew what was coming but was still shocked as Buddy's face shot towards him. It was like throwing a telly off a high-rise building: You know what's going to happen but still flinch when it hits the ground with a bang.

Buddy had loosened his grip. If Ralph could dodge the inevitable impact, he might just make good his escape once full cat-chaos was unleashed.

He dropped to a crouch and scuttled sideways as Buddy's face beat out a sickening percussion against the door. The bass drumbeat of forehead on wood was accompanied by the high-hat bish of shattering glasses with the subtle cracking undertone of breaking nose.

'The fucking midas cat!' shouted a man with a *Gone With the Wind* Rhett Butler moustache. 'The bastard thing's real!'

From his new position under the table, Ralph watched Tony, the acne scarred gang member, take aim at the cat with his knife. 'Jesus, Mary, and all the rest!' Tony's eyes widened as he pulled his arm back. 'It ain't superstition!'

The cat had sprung onto Rhett's shoulder, and Tony loosed his weapon. Didn't they realise? Didn't they know? The midas cat would always be several moves ahead of them and already planning its killing blow.

The blade vanished into Rhett's left upper arm at the exact moment the cat leapt out of sight. Ralph had to smile in spite of his precarious position. They may have been mafia hierarchy, but he was the world's leading midas cat expert. They were dead, and they didn't even know it.

Rhett stared at the knife sticking out of his left arm and, without a sound, slowly drew it out. Ralph knew that if that was him, he'd have been on the carpet, writhing about in screaming agony with damp underpants. God, these blokes were tough bastards.

The spray of blood from the spinning weapon spackled the wall as it left Rhett's hand. 'That's how to throw a knife, motherfucker!'

Ralph hustled around to gain a clearer view. Tony's right hand was pinned Christ-like to the wall, and it looked as though Rhett was about to take full advantage of the situation. Directly or indirectly it was always the same: Wherever the midas cat appeared, pain, suffering and, more often than not, death followed.

Where was the evil little furball, anyway? It had shot out of sight, but he was sure it hadn't left the room.

The almost silent bomp from beside him answered that question. It had materialised on the carpet and was crouched just the other side of the chairs... and it was staring at him. The look it gave him was what? Imploring? The sounds of gang warfare had heightened with hardcore screams and triple-x rated swearing, and the bloody cat was beckoning to him. What did the damned creature want him to do, give himself up to the mafia? How much of a moron did it think he was? He shook his head, but the animal wasn't leaving anytime soon. It had reached a paw towards him, and before he had a chance to pull away, it grabbed his hand. It was going to drag him into the melee.

The softness of the cat's paw belied its strength. It had him in a wrestler-strength grip and was trying to haul him into the open. No. He wasn't going to let it.

Its urgency seemed to increase as it pulled against his resistance. What were the gangsters up to? He glanced behind him. Luckily, they were still going at it and not looking in his direction. Not yet anyway.

The logical part of Ralph's brain broke through the panicked fight-or-flight impulse. If the cat wanted to draw attention to him, it would have been a lot easier just to tap one of the men on the shoulder and point under the table. It hadn't done that, though. It was trying to get him out from his hiding place as quietly as possible. After several years of it trying to kill him, was it trying to redeem itself by saving him?

The odds of him surviving the next round with the cosa nostra were, if he was totally honest, less than not good. So either he trusted the devil's mouser, or he waited to get discovered by a bunch of murderous thugs.

The cat hauled on his arm once again, its pink handbag bouncing on its left hip. This time he came willingly. He crawled from his hiding place, and the cat pointed to the open heating duct high on the wall.

The paw slipped from his hand and the creature hopped onto the chair beneath the ducting. That's when the cat's plan became clear. It was breaking him out through the central heating system. So long as the bad guys didn't see him go, they'd be clueless as to how he'd escaped.

The *I heart New York* hoodie vanished into the hole in the wall. All he had to do was follow without being caught. He stood up intent on making a rapid exit, when his left leg seized solid. He'd been screwed up in a tense bundle under the table for so long, cramp had set in, preventing not only his escape, but any movement at all.

Straightening his leg and shaking it hard, he tried to look in the direction of the fight which was, by the sound of it, reaching its natural conclusion. In about twenty seconds they'd find him standing under the open vent doing the Hokey-Cokey whilst waiting to be whacked.

Big green eyes shone from the ducting as the cat's face reappeared. It had waited for him. It was serious about breaking him out. Well, he'd better not disappoint it.

The screaming and swearing had dropped to whimpers and mutters. That meant he only had a few seconds before whack-time.

He stood on the chair, gripped the hole's edge and, whilst looking over at the men, pulled himself to safety. He'd made it. They hadn't looked round, and as he crawled into the musty darkness, he listened for any sounds of discovery. Nothing. He couldn't believe it. He really did have a chance of getting out of this alive, and it was all due to the midas cat.

The heating tunnel was tight, but so long as it didn't get any narrower, he'd be on a plane back home within the next few hours. He'd be free, but a niggling thought drilled away at the back of his mind. The mafia don't give up. They'd never stop looking for him. There was only one way they'd stop, and that was if they were all dead. Vincenzo would put out a contract on Mickey Eyeball because the men would blame him for destroying the vase. The cat destroyed the vase, though. Was it really saving his life, or was it planning a more gruesome death for him? What to do, though? He could keep following it, or he could pop back and say howdy to Vincenzo and the boys. Some bloody choice! The thing was, though, the cat was worth a hundred million. If he could catch it and offer it to Don Vincenzo, the boss would have something worth more than the Twin-Mings. He'd then have something to offer the triads, and that would make Mickey, AKA himself, a hero. Sorted.

The oppressive dust-caked blackness was lightening ahead of him. He could just make out the pointy-eared outline waiting for him. If it stayed still long enough, he'd be able to grab it.

The only problem was the severe lack of space. The cat was smaller than him and able to move relatively freely in the confines. He, on the other hand, had no choice but to crawl centimetres at a time.

The duct turned a sharp right, and the light flooding in from the vent in the floor, even though it wasn't particularly bright, hurt his eyes.

The creature had hustled to the far side of the grate and wasn't moving. It had a paw to its lips. Was it telling him to be quiet? Why? He shimmied towards the grate. The cat hadn't moved. All he had to be was quick. Reach forward and snatch it, and he'd be able to present Don Vincenzo with one hundred million pounds worth of peace offering.

The only thing between him and non-assassination was the grate. He looked down.

He was peering into a hotel room from above. Standing directly beneath him was a Chinese-looking man in an expensive suit who was holding what appeared to be a machine pistol. That was just typical, wasn't it. He couldn't be peeping into a room with a gorgeous blonde in it, could he? Oh no, *he* had to be the one perched over the triads' New York centre of operations, and the bloke below him looked every inch the boss.

If Ralph made too much noise, what were the chances of not being shot? The Midas cat, though. He'd never been so close to catching it in his life, and his life depended on him catching it.

That gave him only one option. Catch it now.

Easing forwards onto the vent, he reached for the furry prize. The animal was just out of reach and had turned away from him. He lunged for it, but it took off at a sprint, leaving him with his arm outstretched grasping at empty air. The damned thing was setting him up. He was sure of it.

The creak from beneath his knees made him glance down again. The triad boss was looking up, a puzzled expression creasing his forehead into frown lines.

The creak became a series of increasingly loud cracks, and the boss raised his weapon. Ralph tried to get off the vent, but it buckled under his weight, trapping his artificial foot in a decorative piece of filigree metalwork.

The final crack was followed by a feeling of weightlessness, a heavy thumping landing, a terminal-sounding grunt and patters of broken plaster as it rained down into the room.

Ralph was lying on top of the triad boss whose head was at an angle it really shouldn't have been.

Oh, Jesus. The cat *had* set him up. It had made him kill the triad boss. That put him on the triads' radar as well as the mafias'. Ralph wasn't just dead, he was double-dead.

CHAPTER 12

Don Vincenzo

Don Vincenzo checked his watch. They'd had their five minutes. Either they'd give up who'd helped Mickey or give up who'd helped Mickey with a dose of added pain.

'OK, Al,' he said, 'get the door. It's time for some truth-telling.'

The big man reached for the handle and turned it, making way for Vincenzo who stepped into the room.

Vincenzo's right foot hovered above the carpet in an unfinished step. 'What? Who?' In the past three hundred seconds his inner circle of made guys had battered each other, vandalised the main conference suite in the Waldorf Astoria and destroyed the last remaining Ming. His foot came to rest on a crunch of broken ceramics.

'I suppose you bunch of imbeciles had good reason to smash up the suite, each other, and the triads' peace offering.' He folded his arms across his belly. 'Well?' He surveyed the carnage. Tony, Jim and Lou were covered in blood, as was a section of wall that looked as though it had been stabbed. He looked around at the faces once again but could only count six. Someone pivotal to all this shit wasn't in the room. The man responsible for a, what was now inevitable, gang war had vanished. 'Where's Mickey?' he said in what he hoped was a reasonable tone of voice. If he lost it now, he'd start shooting, and who could blame him? He had to keep a lid on his anger, though. If he didn't, he'd no longer have an inner circle.

'Mickey?' Lou put the remaining unbroken Buddy Holly glasses lens to his right eye and looked around the room. 'He's err…'

'Yeah, Lou,' Vincenzo cut in. 'He's err, ain't he?' He felt his pulse-rate rev. His doctor had told him to not get too excited. Too excited? He wasn't excited, though. He was angry, although the word *angry* didn't do his Old Testament-style rage justice. His trigger finger was itching to be put to good use right now, but he knew he had to control himself.

'At least we had one of the Twin-Mings.' He took a deep breath in order to steady the shake in his voice. 'Mr Xao, as I'm sure I've already pointed out, is in the building. You know what that means, don't you?'

The men nodded.

'So I'll ask you one more time. What the fuck happened here, and where's Mickey?'

'It was… was…' Blood dripped from Tony's handkerchief-wrapped right hand that he held in the air.

'What, Tony? What?' The fury had started to surface causing Vincenzo to raise his voice. 'For fuck's sake just speak, you moron!'

'Midas cat.' Tony's face was already a lighter shade of agony but lost the remaining colour as Vincenzo whipped out his silenced nine millimetre.

'The fuck did you say?' Vincenzo's head had started pounding and his chest felt tight. The mere mention of that cursed creature was enough to wipe out everyone in this room and Tony, one of his most trusted men, had the gall to claim that it had been here and caused all this.

He crossed himself before looking to the ceiling. 'Lord deliver us.'

'It came through the vent up there.' Blood flicked onto the wall as Tony pointed at the uncovered ducting. 'It slid on the table and smashed the vase.'

'It did what?' Did Tony expect him to believe that a demon-spawn lived in the Waldorf Astoria's heating system? 'And I suppose it spirited Mickey away through the vent to its demonic lair, did it?'

'I don't know,' said Tony with a shrug. 'Maybe.'

'Maybe?' Vincenzo's barely controlled temper burst free of its constraints. 'Maybe?' he yelled. 'Maybe you should quit trying to curse the entire organisation with your fucking blaspheming!' Before he realised what had happened, three *phuts* spat from his gun and three red blooms flowered on Tony's already blood-flecked white shirt.

Shock and surprise registered briefly before Tony

dropped onto the carpet with the unique finality reserved for the recently dead.

'I don't want to hear another word about the cat-that-must-not-be-named. Do I make myself clear?'

The remaining men murmured and nodded.

'Now. Who can tell me where that bald fuck is?'

Shrugs from the crew confirmed Vincenzo's worst fears. Either they were all in on Mickey's private job, or they were all idiots.

'You really need to find him.' Vincenzo holstered his pistol before looking back to the men. 'He's gonna be sacrificed for the greater good. If I can give him to Xao, maybe I can head off this war.' He looked around the room for a final time. 'Oh and clear this shit up and dispose of that,' he said, pointing at Tony's still form. 'When you find Mickey, I'll be in my room.' He nodded to Al. 'Let's go.'

CHAPTER 13

The Cat

Having backtracked, she stared into the conference room. What the hell was Ralph up to jigging about like that? He didn't have time to do a little dance. The gangsters' yelling and yelping was dying away. It would be a matter of a few seconds, and the entire gaggle of thugs would see Ralph clambering up the wall.

Thankfully, he'd finished doing his mutant version of the can-can and had pulled himself into the hole. All he had to do now was follow her, and he'd be out of the danger zone.

She zigged and zagged through the maze of tunnels, stopping occasionally to make sure Ralph was keeping up. Humans were so slow; it was a wonder they managed to get anything done at all.

After a few more turns, the musty darkness started retreating. She was on the right track because the vent above the Chinaman's room was up ahead.

She hopped across the grille and stopped. There wasn't any point in going on ahead because it was about to get properly black, and humans, unlike the superior feline race, could see none too well in the dark. If Ralph took a wrong turn, there was every chance of him falling into the boiler or ending up back in the roomful of gangsters.

She looked down into the room below. It was that Chinese-looking guy she'd seen earlier, but this time he was holding a weapon of some kind. What was it with this hotel? Was it a magnet for organised crime, or something?

The scuffling racket that echoed down the shaft told her that Ralph was finally catching up. If that dangerous looking bloke heard him, he'd probably shoot him... and her. She looked up again. Ralph was on the far side of the grate. She put a paw to her lips. He had to quieten down if he wanted to get out alive.

He crawled onto the grille and stopped. Good grief! Humans weren't just noisy; they could be incredibly dense as well. He was heavier than her by quite a considerable margin, and she hadn't hung around on the grille any longer than she had to, so what was the dozy plank up to?

He was staring into the room below, for goodness' sake. That's when a terrified expression lit his face up.

Yes, that's right, thought Cat. *You're kneeling directly above a modern day ninja.* Well he'd better start following her soon because if he stayed where he was any longer, he'd be paying the chap a surprise visit.

She turned around and scooted up the metal corridor. Ralph was bound to follow. Well, what other choice did he have?

Now that they were deep in the heating system, Cat decided that it was time to fire up some escape music to help them on their way. Adam Ant's *Dog Eat Dog* was perfect. The solid driving rhythm would help pick her pace up. That meant Ralph would have to stop hanging about, because the bad guys would soon figure out what had happened and be waiting for them at the other end.

Were those creaks coming from her iPod or were they external? If they were external, that meant there was something seriously wrong with the central heating system that she was inside of. If that was the case, then she'd better get to the exit. Ralph would just have to keep up as best he could.

After three, or possibly four, more right turns, the heavy darkness lightened to a dusty glow. She was nearly out. She was almost at the vent the workmen had left open.

Slowing to a walk, she peered ahead at the open grate. Something about it looked familiar and not in a good way. As she edged towards the opening, she saw the chandelier at just above eye level. She was way too high up for this to be the workmen's entrance. That was at floor level. No, she'd made more than one wrong turn, got completely turned around and ended up back at the conference suite.

She killed the music and strained to pick up the slightest sound. There was no fighting, arguing or talking. Apart from the background huff of warm air, she couldn't hear anything.

Switching to stealth-mode, she eased towards the opening and looked down into the suite. Apart from the hole in the wall where the knife had gone in, there was no evidence of the earlier kerfuffle. No blood, no smashed pottery, nothing. Nothing and nobody. One thing she could say in favour of the mafia was their efficiency. That kind of clean-up operation would have taken her days. Whatever. It just meant she could escape without having to backtrack through the ducting. The last place the gangsters would search would be the scene of the crime.

She turned around and beckoned to Ralph, only there *was* no Ralph. The plank had failed to keep up. She just hoped he wasn't inside the boiler. Hopefully, he'd gone the right way and got out safely. Still, there was no point worrying about that now, was there?

Dropping down onto the carpet, she made her way as quietly as she could over to the door. She placed an ear to the cool wood, held her breath and listened. There were no sounds of fighting from the far side. That didn't mean there was nobody there, though. What if the mafia were waiting for her? She lay flat on the floor and peered under the door. No polished gangster shoes and no tell-tale shadows meant that there was a good chance that she was in the clear. Nonetheless, she only opened the door a crack. The corridor was deserted apart from the table with the old vase on it that she'd liberated earlier. There was still no Ralph, though. Wherever he was now was no longer her problem. There was only so much a cat could do.

She took a final look around. That old vase had gone totally un-noticed. If nobody noticed it, nobody would miss it. It wasn't as if it belonged to the hotel in the first place. She was the one who'd put it there, so logic dictated that she could un-put it there. Besides, she had a use for it.

She tucked the flowers out of sight under the table, nestled the ancient ceramic back in her bag and re-entered the room. After all the excitement, it was time for a bit of relaxation, and what better way to relax than with one of the cigars she'd found in the other hotel?

Digging into her capacious handbag, she pulled out the bundle and examined it. The cigars were tied together with what looked like fuse wire, and each one had a length of the same sort of wire sticking out the end. Maybe they were a special limited edition from Cuba? Whatever.

She took a final peep into the corridor to make sure no staff were nearby. If she got caught smoking indoors, she'd probably end up in prison. Seeing no one, she slipped back into the suite, spun the wheel of her zippo, touched the flame to the fuse and inhaled.

Instead of the rich aroma and heady blast of hand-rolled tobacco, a light sputtering fizz was accompanied by the bitter-sweet smell of what could only be described as firework touch-paper. That was just typical. She'd trousered a bundle of joke shop smokes. A squib in the end of the damned thing would probably go off with an underwhelming pop and cover her in a cloud of ground up soot.

The cigar crackled and died which was just as well, really. She'd have enjoyed watching the thing go off, but she had things to do.

She'd just slung the dud cigars under the table in disgust when the quiet click of the door latch made her look up. Someone was coming in. She'd never get out through the vent in time. Hiding was the only option. If she slipped in behind the door as it opened, she might get away with it. The door opened. She hadn't moved. It was too late. She froze as a group of Chinese men in the sharpest of silk suits entered. She was halfway between the table and the door, with a bunch of triads staring down at her.

She did the only thing she could think of and waved at them. Perhaps a friendly greeting would put them off their stride?

One of the men smiled, so Cat continued waving.

'Lucky cat.' The man holstered the pistol he'd been carrying before turning to face his comrades. Whatever it was they were talking about must have been something nice, because each of them patted Cat's head as they passed her.

The sound of chairs being moved made Cat look round. The Chinamen were seated at the table and had started talking in low voices. If she slipped out right now, they'd never notice.

Popping in her earbuds, she pulled her hood over her Yankees baseball cap and, without checking to see if the coast was clear, shot out into the corridor and jogged towards the elevator.

The Jimmy Choo shoebox that sat outside the hotel room door was obviously empty. Well, who would leave a pair of shoes with that kind of price tag just lying around? Scooping up the box told her everything she needed to know. Yes it was empty, and yes she had a use for it. It was perfect, in fact.

The lift pinged, and the door slid open disgorging an impossible number of people. It was still way too packed, though. It was healthier taking the stairs, anyway. More fun too, especially if she slid down the bannisters.

CHAPTER 14

Ralph

Ralph was lying on top of a dead triad: A triad he'd just killed. OK, it wasn't on purpose, but who the hell was going to believe him? He was what, taking a stroll through the heating system and accidentally fell through a vent, breaking this bloke's neck? Oh, and don't forget his uncanny resemblance to a member of the mafia whose face was splurged all over the media.

Plaster crunched as he rolled off the body onto the floor. He hadn't lost his foot, and it didn't feel as if anything was broken. That was a bonus. What negated his lack of breakages, however, had a head that faced the wrong way, and a deadly organisation that would do the same to him, if they caught up with him.

He sat up and eyed the machine pistol that lay on the carpet. He'd seen enough movies to know it was a Mac 10, but not enough to know how the bloody thing worked. When faced with the possibility of actually firing it, could he? Even if he could, he'd probably do more damage to himself or leave the safety on. No, it was best he left it alone.

Scrambling to his feet, he dusted off the bits of ceiling that still clung to him. He had to leave. Not just the hotel or New York, he had to leave the States. He had to leave now.

As he reached for the door handle, voices from outside stopped him from grasping it. Whoever it was, wasn't speaking English or Italian. They were speaking Chinese, and they were getting nearer.

His pulse beat out a tattoo in his temples. It was bad enough being discovered in a hotel room with a dead body. When that body belonged to a triad, an extremely slow death involving fast-growing bamboo was the only thing he'd have to look forward to. He'd entered through the ceiling vent. If he stood on a chair, he'd still never reach it. Even if he could, the Ralph-shaped hole would be an obvious first look for the gangsters.

The handle clunked down. Escaping was no longer an option. That only left hiding, but where? The wardrobe in the bedroom? No. That was the first place Michael Myers looked in Halloween. Behind the shower curtain? That was Norman Bates, but what other choice did he have?

The door was opening. He had to move. Luckily, the bathroom door was squeakless, and as he eased it shut behind him, the Chinese voices exploded into what was, no doubt, a whole bunch of swearing.

Furniture was being moved. That meant the men were checking the heating ducts. Once they'd discovered they were Ralphless, what then? They'd search the bedroom and bathroom, that's what.

It wouldn't matter how far down in the bath he huddled because once they'd pulled back the shower curtain, it would be pretty bloody obvious that it wasn't empty. Well, duh!

The only thing he had going for him was there being no CCTV inside the heating system. Nobody knew he was there. If he could get out of the bathroom window before the men came in, he'd be in with a chance.

The hotel was classic thirties art deco. It was probably listed, meaning original windows that opened fully. OK, he was three floors up, it was snowing, and he was scared of heights. His choice was simple, though; fall to a terrifying but quick death, or be tortured to a horrifically slow one instead.

The window had secondary glazing but was, thankfully, original pre-war, and it reached from the bath's rim to the ceiling.

Pushing it wide, he watched the piled snow drop to the street below. He may only have been on the third floor, but he'd still be pizza if he hit the sidewalk. He'd end up as baby food if he didn't go, though.

The Chinese swearing was getting louder. They'd sussed that he wasn't in the heating. They were coming to check the bathroom. It was time to leave.

The ledge was maybe thirty centimetres wide; a foot in old money. That was wide enough to walk along without the risk of falling if he was only a couple of feet off the ground. When the ground was three storeys away, that altered things considerably. Throw in heaped soft snow undercoated with a layer of ice, airborne flakes, a gusting wind and season with armed criminals. Turn up the adrenaline setting to maximum and wait for heartrate to start boiling.

There was no point escaping out the window only to leave it open, though. He gripped the metal frame and eased it shut.

'Oh f-fuck!' The cold bit hard, rattling Ralph's teeth. What the hell was he doing? He was outside the Waldorf Astoria on the third floor having just survived a near-death-experience, and he was about to freeze. He could still feel his fingers, but for how much longer? Shuffling along the ledge, he'd pulled on two windows so far without success. If he didn't find an open window soon, hyperthermia would set in, numbing everything. Balance depended on feeling. No feeling equalled no balance. No balance equalled splat.

A gust of wind sandblasted his face with stinging whiteness, shoving him against the side of the building and twisting his false foot inwards. This was not the time for his ankle bolt to work loose. If he didn't straighten his prosthetic and tighten it up, he'd be taking a parachute-free skydive.

He always carried a screwdriver. Always. When he

lifted his foot, though, it was usually indoors whilst seated in a comfy chair. If he bent down up here, he'd overbalance and die. If he didn't, he'd overbalance and... ditto.

Digging a hand into his inside jacket pocket, he pulled out the little screwdriver. He was losing feeling in his fingers. He had to be quick. Drop the tool, and he may as well follow it over the edge.

If he shuffled sideways and bent down, his bum wouldn't push against the wall, and he wouldn't plunge to the snow-bound sidewalk. That was the theory, anyway.

With nothing to hold onto, any movement was potentially life-ending, and as he swivelled his good right foot, his inward facing left slid out from under him. With his left leg dangling over a three-storey drop, his balance shifted radically. A breath of wind would be all that was needed to tip him into oblivion. Fingernails scraped on stone as he scrambled for a handhold. There was nothing. He was going to die. He was going to die, and it was all that damned cat's fault.

He had to pull his leg back in and rebalance himself. He was tipping, though. A centimetre more and that would be it; whoops, waa, splat!

His left arm flailed along with his leg. The traffic police had it all wrong. It wasn't speed that killed, it was the sudden stop that did it.

He lunged forwards in a final attempt, and his hand locked onto a metal window frame. It was open. This was his chance. Lose his handhold, though, and it would all be over.

He pulled his left leg back in and bent to straighten his foot. He wasn't going anywhere until he'd sorted that out.

Now his prosthesis was on straight, he could haul himself to safety, apologise to whoever was in the room and catch the next plane home.

He pulled the window wide enough to enter and stepped onto the inner sill. The curtains were drawn, but that didn't matter. If he lost his balance tumbling into the room, the furthest he could fall was about three feet, and he'd be wrapped in nicely padded drapery.

Stepping off the sill, he gripped the thick material. The floor was further away than he thought, and he fell forwards, curtain hooks ping-pinging as they tore free. He was so relieved to be inside and alive, that getting entangled in heavy duty velvet and landing with a thump on the carpet was not even an irritation.

Hands grappled with the drapes. Someone was unwrapping him. He'd have a bit of explaining to do once he was freed, but what the hell. He was alive.

'Oh hi,' he said. 'I...' Whatever he was about to say evaporated with an unwelcome blast of recognition.

There was a pistol, a chubby hand, and a stubby arm that connected to a human beachball.

'Vincenzo?'

CHAPTER 15

Don Vincenzo

'What the hell's going on, Al?' Don Vincenzo's stomach gurgled. The stress of a string of disasters was turning his, already health-food ravaged, digestive system to water.

'First one of the Twin-Mings gets lifted, then Mickey vanishes, only to turn up again with some stupid limey accent.' A deep *gloop-gloop-gloop* bubbled up from underneath Vincenzo's belt. 'Jesus, Al!' Vincenzo looked from his bodyguard to the ceiling and crossed himself before continuing. 'The second Ming gets smashed, Mickey disappears again, and the men start talking about the-cat-that-must-not-be-named. Have I missed anything out?'

'Err, the triads, Boss.'

'Like I could forget Xao, and his gaggle of maniacs.' He pulled out his vaper, stared at it and stuffed it back into his pocket. He needed a hit on a Cohiba, not a lemon drizzle cake scented fake smoke. 'We have to find Mickey.' He'd started pacing again without realising. When his stomach connected with the hotel room's bedroom door, he spun to face Al once again. 'If the one-eyed boom-bug doesn't show, we're either gonna have to sacrifice another made guy, or...or...' Vincenzo didn't have a clue how to finish the sentence. Or...what? Honour had to be satisfied. As head of The Family, he understood this better than most. No Mings, no Mickey, no peace offering, no plan C.

Mickey had blabbed about the-cat-that-must-not-be-named, though. So had Tony, God rest his sorry-ass soul. Shit, was the furry demon real? If it was, it would explain a whole load.

'Do you believe in curses, Al?'

Al shrugged, 'I guess so. I curse all the time.'

'Dammit, Al!'

'Yeah.' Al held up a finger, 'And *shit*, and if I hit my thumb with a hammer, I usually yell *motherfucker*. That last one's a good one.'

'Not that kind of curse.' Vincenzo seriously wondered if Al hadn't fallen out of his pram and head-butted concrete when he was a baby. 'The biblical kind. You know; boils, locusts; that sort of thing.'

Al nodded slowly as if trying to decipher the last sentence. 'Err, well... I go to mass every Sunday, and the priest says they're real. Priests always tell the truth, so that means I have to believe in them.'

'Exactly, Al. Exactly.' Vincenzo snapped his fingers. 'Two of the men claim to have seen the demon feline, and the entire plan to head off a war has been flushed.'

The floor to ceiling velvet curtains rippled as a hard snow-bearing wind sung through the gap in the just-open window. Stress always pushed Vincenzo's temperature up, and he needed the cold air to help him think straight. What he didn't need, though, was a face full of melting slush, so the drapes remained shut.

They rippled again, before bulging inwards. Vincenzo frowned as the bulge became person-shaped. Curtain hooks twanged as they snapped from the rings. Somebody was coming in through the outside window from three floors up.

The bundle hit the carpet with a dull, but solid, thump. He was about to discover Batman's true identity. Not without protection, though.

Whipping out the nine millimetre with his right hand, he tore at the velvet with his left.

'Oh hi, I...' Melting snow still clung to the pinstripe suit, and the man's eyebrows and lashes were frosted white.

'Vincenzo?'

And he was still talking in that Dick Van Dyke, Mary Poppins voice.

'Al!' Mickey Eyeball had just flown in, possibly preventing a gang war. First things first, though. 'Get the prick into a chair. There are things he needs to tell us before I present him to Xao.'

'Wh-whiskey.' Vincenzo felt like pistol whipping

the myopic maniac for scaring all the saints out of him, and he was asking for scotch?

'Oh no, no, no.' He wagged a finger at the shivering wreck. 'I need answers to questions like; where's the second Ming? And where's my fifteen percent cut of all the private work you've been doing? And what's the last one? Oh yeah. What, in the name of Holy Mary, Mother of God, were you doing outside my window, on the third floor?' He hammered the last query home. The first couple of questions should have had fairly straight forward explanations. Flying around a hundred, or so, feet up in the air, however, not so much.

'Ch-Chinese gang leader.' Vincenzo's large intestine loosened with a deep, echoey glop. He needed the bathroom, but he needed to hear what Mickey *Batman* Eyeball had to say about Xao. Whatever it was, he knew it wasn't going to be good.

'What about him?'

'He's d-d-dead.'

'Dead?' If Mickey killed Xao, they were all dead, or would be in the coming few hours. 'Dead how?'

'Cats are lucky in Ch-China.' Melted snow puddled under Mickey's chair making it look as if he'd pissed himself. Maybe he had? He wasn't going to sniff it to find out, though.

'Yeah, I know. So fucking what?' He hoped the interrogation wasn't heading in the direction he thought it was.

'I was following the midas cat through the heating ducts. I was trying to catch it. It's worth a hundred million. Give it to the triads as a peace offering. I made a grab for it and fell through a vent onto the triad boss, breaking his neck.'

The-cat-that-must-not-be-named. Everything came down to that ungodly ball of fur.

'Never, and I mean never, ever mention that satanic creature in my presence again! Am I being heard?' He had to keep a tight hold on his anger, or he'd end up killing the peace offering, and Xao's men would want to do that themselves. He couldn't see anything but all-out war, though.

'But it *was* the midas cat!'

He had to, didn't he? He just couldn't keep his fake limey accent clammed for even one second.

The *phut* from the silenced pistol was followed immediately by the splintering of foot bones and Mickey's yelp. Mickey wasn't dead, but he'd have something to keep his mind occupied instead of the hairy demon spawn.

'Oh, Jesus!' Mickey leapt out of his chair and scuttled backwards into the wall. 'I'm not Mickey! I'm not Mickey!'

Vincenzo's brain did its thing whilst Mickey cowered against the wood panelling. The Irish pyro managed to steal the vase from the limo without being seen, he vanishes before re-appearing talking Limey. Then he disappears from a locked room before flying in through a window on the third floor. So far, so weird.

'I'm not Mickey!'

'Shut up, I'm thinking!' Vincenzo's gaze dropped

to Mickey's shattered appendage, and the weirdness level went into overdrive. Not only was there no blood, Mickey was still upright. Well, sort of upright. OK, he was crouched up against the wall with his arms over his head, but the pertinent point was the fact that he was bearing weight on a blasted foot without any obvious discomfort. Vincenzo knew what a gunshot wound felt like; he'd had enough of his own over the years. When you've been shot in the foot, you tended to roll around on the floor, howling in agony. Mickey wasn't. No blood, no pain, and he knew about the-cat-that-must-not-be-named. Oh, Holy Father. It all added up. The cursed feline had turned Mickey into a vampire.

That's when a new plan presented itself. The bald nutjob kept saying he wasn't Mickey. Well of course he wasn't. He was Mickey's re-animated corpse. He was, pretty much, immortal. Sacrifice him to the triads, and as long as they kept him out of the daylight and didn't poke sharpened sticks through his heart, he'd be able to wipe out the entire organisation.

'Mickey, Mickey, Mickey.' This new plan now made Mr Eyeball Vincenzo's new Number Two. Hell, if he worked things right, Mickey O'Dracula could help him become New York's next mayor.

'All is forgiven, my friend. I've just got a little job for you.' He turned to face Al. 'Pour Mr Eyeball a scotch.' He didn't know whether vampires could drink, or not. Mickey had asked for whiskey when he'd appeared, though, so they probably could.

'Can't you see the man's freezing.'

CHAPTER 16

Ralph

He'd escaped from the triads by clambering out onto a three-storey-high ledge, only to climb into Don Vincenzo's room. With high odds, if you needed something good to happen, it wouldn't, but if you needed something bad not to happen, it would.

'Al!' Vincenzo's gun hand was shaking, and his face wasn't reddening, it was purpling.

'Get the prick into a chair. There are things he needs to tell us before I present him to Xao.'

Hands the size of banana bunches gripped Ralph under the arms and threw him into a dining chair.

'Wh-whiskey.' Five minutes out on the ledge had flash-frozen him. He needed a quick thaw if he was going to have any chance of survival.

'Oh no, no, no.' Vincenzo wagged a stubby finger in his face. 'I need answers to questions like; where's the second Ming? And where's my fifteen percent cut of all the private work you've been doing? And what's the last one? Oh yeah. What, in the name of Holy Mary, Mother of God, were you doing outside my window, on the third floor?'

Vincenzo jabbed the pistol forwards as he accentuated the last four words. Ralph didn't have an answer for the first two questions. The last one, though, was all down to… 'Ch- Chinese gang leader.'

Vincenzo's facial colour scheme was like one of those old mood rings. Purple faded to red and morphed to pink before finally settling on a pale greenie-grey, and his innards let out an unsettling gurgle.

'What about him?'

'He's d-d-dead.'

'Dead? Dead how?'

Dead how? Dead because of the midas cat, that's how. He had to be careful how he phrased his answer, though. One wrong word and the psychotic beachball would start shooting.

'Cats are lucky in Ch-China.'

Vincenzo shrugged. 'Yeah, I know. So fucking what?'

He'd arrived at the critical point in the story. This was where the first shot could ring out. If he stayed silent, though, there was a good chance he'd end up just as dead.

'I was following the midas cat through the heating ducts.' This was it. He'd started now. This conversation had no pause or rewind. 'I was trying to catch it. It's worth a hundred million.' Things had gone well; he hadn't died. 'Give it to the triads as a peace offering. I made a grab for it and fell through a vent onto the triad boss, breaking his neck.'

When he was at school, Ralph had been taught that no harm would come to you if you told the truth. They lied. Don *Beachball* Vincenzo went back through the spectrum, eyes popping in his overstuffed aubergine face.

'Never, and I mean never, ever mention that satanic creature in my presence again! Am I being heard?'

'But it *was* the midas cat!' Why did he have to say that? If he'd have kept his mouth shut, Vincenzo wouldn't be pointing the weapon at his left foot. There was no time for fear as Vincenzo pulled the trigger. The dog-like yelp wasn't him, was it? He didn't know he could make a noise like that. The fat lunatic had just blasted a hole in his prosthetic foot. Next time it would probably be his kneecap. 'Oh, Jesus!' He leapt from his chair and scuttled backwards until he hit the wall.

Al stood mountain-tall and mountain-impassive behind Vincenzo who was quaking like a human volcano.

This whole thing was just a massive misunderstanding. He was an ex-banker, not a gangster, even though he'd been called one from time to time. He had to make Vincenzo see the truth before the psycho started shooting again.

'I'm not Mickey!' The headline photo said otherwise, but he had to try.

'Shut up,' said Vincenzo, 'I'm thinking.'

Thinking? That couldn't mean anything good. Ralph's body went into automatic reflex mode and he curled into as tight a ball as possible, arms over his head. Reality told him that it didn't matter how small he made himself; one bullet would be enough.

'Mickey, Mickey, Mickey.'

Confusion slapped Ralph around the face. He looked up. Vincenzo's voice had become... cosy? Something had just happened but what?

'All is forgiven, my friend.'

Did Vincenzo just call him *my friend?*

'I've just got a little job for you.' Vincenzo faced Al. 'Pour Mr Eyeball a scotch. Can't you see the man's freezing?'

Ralph downed the drink in one, warmth spreading through his system, instead of down his inside leg.

'We've got a meeting to attend,' said Vincenzo with a smile that Ralph couldn't quite de-cipher. It wasn't exactly smug, but it wasn't carefree happiness, either.

'And we need your expertise.'

Ralph nodded. Going to a meeting wasn't so bad. He'd gone to, and hosted, hundreds and was still alive. This was a mafia boss, though. It probably wasn't *that* sort of meeting.

The last time he had visited the conference suite, it hadn't gone at all well. Here he was again, though, outside the same suite, standing in the same puddle of water, but this time there was no vase on the little side table, only a bunch of flowers propped up underneath it.

When Vincenzo reached for the door handle, however, it turned before he'd even touched it, and the door slowly opened.

When a child-sized person wearing an *I Heart NY* hoodie shot out, Ralph knew he was saved from the *meeting*. He didn't see the kid's face, but the pink handbag sealed it for him. That was the midas cat. Catch it and make it tell Don Vincenzo the truth; what happened to the triad boss, the broken vase, even his true identity: Everything. The bloody animal probably knew where the other vase was, as well. Truth be told, the cat had most likely nicked it in the first place.

'The midas cat!' He pointed down the corridor. It was skipping towards the elevator at the far end. If he ran after it with his prosthetic foot shot to hell, he'd faceplant the carpet. It was definitely the cat, though; Adam Ant was playing through its earbuds.

'I told you not to...'

Ralph waved a hand and cut Vincenzo off. 'It's there. Don't let it get away. A hundred million dollar peace offering. Catch it!'

Vincenzo barked an order at Al, and in Ralph's opinion, it was the wrong order.

'Stay with Mickey! To hell with the curse. Let the Chinese have it.'

Ralph had never seen a human beachball run before, and he wasn't seeing one now, either. Vincenzo could barely make it above a fast walk, and he was trying to catch a cat. The fastest animal on the planet was a cat.

The damned creature even had time to stop and pick up what looked like a shoebox, before heading for the lift. Christ on a pedalo! If he didn't do something, he'd never be free of the mafia.

'Al, why don't you go after it?'
Al's brow didn't even crease. He didn't have to think before answering, because his response was pre-programmed.

'I got orders. I stay here with you.'
How the hell did the cosa nostra get to be so powerful if they were all as thick as this bloke?

The elevator pinged and people piled out before the doors were even fully open. Vincenzo had stopped, and the cat had vanished into the near-stampeding mob of Christmas shoppers.

If Al had taken chase instead, they'd probably have a hundred million dollar furry bundle ready to hand over to the Chinese by now. Instead, they had nothing but a horizontal Vincenzo, as a woman, blinded by a head-high stack of gift-wrapped boxes, walked straight into him. He'd had nowhere to go, as his bulk prevented any rapid counter measures. The scurrying hoards had hemmed him in as they squeezed past on either side, and Ralph flinched as the inevitable head-on unfolded.

Pushed by the crowd behind her, the woman hit Vincenzo, letting out a siren-squeal as her present stack became airborne along with Vincenzo as he tumbled gracelessly backwards.

In normal circumstances he would have found the whole scene hilarious. In normal circumstances there wouldn't have been a threat of gang warfare, though.

Vincenzo had landed on the carpet, and the woman had landed on Vincenzo. The deflating balloon sound could only have been Vincenzo's colon forcing out an illegal quantity of greenhouse gasses. The squelchy finish, however, suggested something not quite gaseous, and not quite solid.

Once the crowd had dispersed, it was obvious the cat had escaped.

'I'm so sorry.' The woman had climbed off Vincenzo and was busy herding boxes. 'I didn't see you there, I...' She gagged. Vincenzo's methane eruption had probably hit home.

The woman jog-walked as fast as her box-skyscraper would allow. 'Sorry about your friend,' she said as she hurried up the corridor. 'I think he needs a bath.'

Any thoughts of escape fled as the rest of the Reservoir Dogs rounded the corner.

'Hey, Al,' said Buddy Holly, his gaffa-taped glasses perching on a swollen band-aided nose. 'Why's the boss on the floor?'

'I'm having a little rest before the meeting.' Vincenzo heaved his not insubstantial bulk upright before flopping back down, the odour of loaded underpants filling the hallway.

When nobody came to his aid, he let out a frustrated sounding sigh. 'Will somebody please lend a hand here?'

'Phew,' said Buddy, 'what's that smell?'

'Three months of salad, muesli, pure orange juice and no Cohibas!' Vincenzo almost screamed the last two words. He scrambled to his feet and waddled over to Ralph. 'You said that kid was the-cat-that-must-not-be-named.' He prodded Ralph in the chest with a doughy sausage forefinger. 'I never saw its face, so how do I know you're not pulling some kind of stunt?'

Ralph never saw its face either, but the build, the size, the pink handbag, and the fact that it came out of the conference suite were strong pieces of circumstantial evidence.

'I know it was the m...' Ralph bit off the end of the sentence. If he mentioned the creature by name, Vincenzo would probably shoot him again. This time in his good foot, and that wouldn't be pleasant. 'I know it was the-cat-that-must-not-be-named, because, as I've said before; I've seen it up close.'

'Err, Boss.' The gangster that reminded Ralph of Rhett Butler raised his hand as if he were in school. 'Hadn't we better get into the meeting before the Chinese arrive?'

Vincenzo nodded, his aubergine tinted face fading back to its usual pallor. 'Yeah, you're right.'

As soon as Vincenzo entered the room, the kersnick of at least half a dozen weapons being cocked told Ralph that the Chinese had arrived at the party early.

'Hello, Don Vincenzo.' The voice from the other side of the closed door was definitely East Asian. 'Tell your men to enter.'

CHAPTER 17

Don Vincenzo

'Hello, Don Vincenzo.'

Vincenzo was so pre-occupied with his squishy underpants, it took him a moment to comprehend his situation.

'Tell your men to enter.' Unsmiling Chinese in tailored silk suits had missile-lock on him. If he moved just a fraction too quick, the machine-pistols would unzip him.

'Hi, fellas.' He held his hands in front of him, palms out, fingers splayed. 'Now, I don't know what's going on any more than you do.' He had to play for time. He also had to get a message to his guys. They walk in here, they die, and the New York mafia dies with them.

'Xao dead.' The tallest of the dozen, or so, men sniffed the air, his implacable expression collapsing into disgust.

Vincenzo had loaded his underpants, and it was all down to the-cat-that-must-not-be-named. Luckily, he was wearing a dark suit. If anyone mentioned the smell, though, he'd blame it on the plumbing.

'Yeah, I heard.' That was the second triad Mickey had a hand in killing. Fucking Mickey! Fucking *vampire* Mickey. Fucking *immortal* Mickey. His gastric accident plus a roomful of guns trained on him had pushed the plan clean out of his head. Only thing was, it needed a rapid re-think. Rapid to the point of right now. If only the damned cat-that-must-not-be-named hadn't shown up. He smiled at the men. He'd just thought of a plan. Its success was maybe slim-to-zero, but he had no other idea, or choice.

'In your culture, cats are considered lucky, yes?'

The taller of the crew, who was obviously the new leader, nodded and frowned before looking frantically around the room as if he'd lost something. 'Lucky cat gone.'

So it *was* true. The kid that exited earlier really was the hundred million dollar devil spawn.

'Yeah,' said Vincenzo. 'Lucky cat gone but not far.' Now was the time for care, for patience, for finesse. 'Lucky cat was in here earlier, yes?'

The man nodded.

'Now it's gone, yes?'

Another nod.

'You've heard of the...' It could now go one of two ways. Either the midas cat was a blessing, or a curse '...midas cat, yes?'

Another nod, eyes widening. He wasn't dead, so hopefully the cat was considered mega lucky. OK, he didn't actually *have* the animal, but these guys didn't know that.

'It's wearing an *I heart NY* hoodie, and it's carrying a pink handbag. Am I right?' It was just as well he'd seen it shoot out of the room.

More nodding.

'You just let the midas cat slip through your fingers, my friend. But don't worry. We have it in a safe place.'

'A safe place?'

'That's right.' Vincenzo smiled in what he hoped was a reassuring manner. 'We have the luckiest cat on the planet secured just for you.' He looked at his outstretched hands before jutting one of his chins towards the weapons. 'I don't think there's any need for those, eh?'

The leader lowered his gun and gestured for the rest to do likewise.

'I'm going to call in my guys now. I'll tell them to holster their guns. I mean, we're all friends here.'

'They come in now,' said the leader. 'They come in slowly with hands up.'

'Fair enough,' said Vincenzo as he opened the door. 'Guys, I need you to stow your hardware, and come in slowly with hands raised. We have guests, and we need to show them respect.' Should he have Mickey come in first or last, though? His secret weapon should fight a rear-guard action. Yes, that was a good plan. Always leave the best 'til last. 'Oh, and Al? Send in Mickey last.'

The made guys filed in, hands raised just as a faint fizzing hiss issued from under the conference table. The familiar bitter-sweet aroma was unmistakable, and he wondered how long he had until the bomb went off.

'Oh no! I'm not going in there!' Mickey was screaming in his faux London accent. It sounded as though Al was having trouble.

The door flew open and Al's bulk came into view. It was obvious to Vincenzo that Al was having a tug-of-war with the myopic maniac.

'I'm having problems, Boss.'

None of that mattered anymore, though, did it? He had to get his guys out of the room before they were all smithereened. 'Everybody out! There's a bomb under the...'

Light travels a lot faster than sound. Vincenzo knew this as an absolute fact, so when the flash that wiped out his vision was followed a nanosecond later by the blast, he wasn't surprised. This was his last ever thought.

CHAPTER 18

Ralph

Ralph could feel the tension gripping the mobsters almost as much as he could feel Al's fingers digging into his upper arm. The last thirty seconds had elasticated into what felt like an hour. Vincenzo was negotiating with a roomful of men that wanted him dead, and it sounded as though he was winning them over. He had to admit a grudging respect for the fat psychopath. He'd just told the triads that he had the midas cat in captivity. When the triads discovered the ruse, what then?

'They come in now,' said the stand-in triad leader. 'They come in with hands up.'

They come in now meant *he* come in now. Vincenzo had said that he had a job for him. He hadn't been told what that job was, but Ralph had more than a sneaking suspicion it had something to do with what the Chinese would call an honourable death. *His* honourable death. He didn't want to die; honourably or otherwise. He just wanted to go home.

'Fair enough,' said Vincenzo, and the door to the conference suite opened.

That was it. Ralph knew his chances of seeing out the next five minutes had evaporated. Enter the room, kneel down and blam! He wouldn't get to see the walls redecorated in brain-matter grey.

He held his ground as Al took up the slack.

'Guys,' said Vincenzo, 'I need you to stow your hardware and come in slowly with your hands raised. We have guests, and we need to show them respect.'

Vincenzo had walked into an ambush having just shat himself and came out, not exactly rose-scented; not literally at any rate, but with a whole load more leverage than when he went in.

'Oh, and Al?' said Vincenzo, 'send Mickey in last.'

Vincenzo had singled him out. The plebs always get executed first, leaving royalty as the headline act. Oh, Jesus! Those order-followers were marching to their deaths, and he was the star act.

When a fireworky scent drifted from the room, he understood. The mafia weren't in charge, and neither were the triads. It was the cat. The bloody thing had planted a bomb meaning to obliterate everyone.

Al tugged on Ralph's arm, but Ralph dug in hard.

'Oh no! I'm not going in there!' Al had Ralph in both hands and was dragging him towards the door.

'I'm having problems, Boss.'

Damned right he was having problems. The hell-tabby meant to blow up the conference suite and everyone in it. So long as he stayed away from the door, he might just live.

'Everybody out!' yelled Vincenzo. 'There's a bomb under the...'

The world shook as the blast shotgunned outwards, blowing the door, and Al, up against the opposite wall.

His ears rang as dust and debris settled on and around him. If he hadn't resisted Al's tugging, he'd have been in the path of the explosion, and as dead as Al was right now. The big guy was definitely dead; he had a splintered chair leg sticking out of his face. That meant that everybody else had to have been unalive as well. That meant he was free of organised crime. The bloody cat had inadvertently saved his life.

He wasn't sure if he should be grateful to the tabby-from-hell or not. It had destroyed one of the Mings, set him up to kill the triad boss and very nearly blown him up. If he hadn't resisted Al's tugging, he'd had been standing by the door, maybe even in the room, instead of by the wall which shielded him from the blast.

From somewhere way beyond his explosion-induced tinnitus came what he assumed to be the hotel's fire alarm. He was probably the only survivor of what the papers would no doubt call a terrorist attack. If he was the sole survivor, that would place him front and centre as the bomber. He was in no mood to answer awkward questions; especially given his uncanny resemblance to a well-known safe cracker who favoured dynamite.

He eyed the lift. No, it was no use going that way. In the event of a fire, always use the stairs. The only problem with that was the fire brigade, bomb squad and NYPD piling up them. He didn't have a choice, though. It was the stairs or nothing. How long would it take the police to arrive in a snowstorm? Five, ten minutes? He looked around. There were rooms on this floor. Rooms with people in. They'd be opening their doors to see what the hell was going on. No, scrap that. They'd be opening their doors to escape from the fire that was spreading through the conference suite. The corridor lights had been blown out by the blast, but he could see perfectly well because of the dancing orange glow shining through the jagged hole that was once the suite's doorway.

Al's blood and dust-caked face looked not only alive but suntanned and healthy in the firelight. Well, as healthy as he could look with a chair leg sticking out of his face.

He stumbled towards the stairs. He must have looked like a war zone victim. If anyone saw him, they'd remember him. *Yes, that was him, all right. The bald bloke in a gangster suit. He was covered in dust and blood and was legging it down Broadway.* He had to find a toilet before anyone saw him. Jam the door and get cleaned up.

Luckily, the stairs were empty, but as he burst out into the lobby, he was met by a scene of utter chaos. It was just as well people didn't pay attention to safety instructions, otherwise the morons piling out of the elevators would have all been on the stairs, and he would have been in the back of a police cruiser by now.

The crush of people were stampeding towards the exit just as the fire fighters were trying to get in, and in the confusion nobody paid him any attention whatsoever. He still had to clean up, though, because he was the only one looking like he'd been at the epicentre of the blast.

Slipping into the gents, he checked the cubicles: Empty. So far, so getting away with it. All he had to do now was get himself cleaned up and follow the herd out onto the streets.

The man staring out of the mirror was a shell-shocked whiteface clown, but thankfully not blood spattered. Once the dust had been washed off, that just left a terror stricken nobody in a rumpled pinstriped suit.

The crowds had thinned considerably by the time he left the restroom, and he walked as fast as he could towards the exit without drawing attention to himself. When he heard his name called out, he almost vomited. He swallowed hard, forcing the bile back down his gullet. It was *his* name, though, and not Mickey Eyeball's. Somebody knew who he was. He considered sprinting for the door, but of course his shattered artificial foot wouldn't allow it. He'd take a dive after the first few steps. If he ignored the call, maybe whoever was after him might assume they'd got him mixed up with someone else. Who, though? A gangster named Mickey?

'Mister Ralph.'

There it was again. He kept walking.

'Mister Ralph. Sir?'

Sir? Through the din of sirens, and the general hubbub of the evacuation, Ralph recognised the sound of hotel professionalism. Sure, the cops called people *sir*, but not in that particular manner. That was hotel-speak, not cop-speak. He stopped walking, turned and faced the voice. The concierge was waving at him from behind the desk.

'Mister Ralph.' The man's urgency levels were spiking. There was no way Ralph was getting away unnoticed. If he kept walking, he'd probably get chased. It was time to face whatever fate was going to dump on him. He fought his way through the cross-flow of people, the odours of expensive perfumes and aftershaves mingling with the tang of smoke and scent of panic.

'Yeah?' he said when he reached the desk. 'I'm Ralph. What do you want?' He wasn't usually that snippy, but he'd had a bit of a bad day and wasn't up for polite chit chat.

'Mister Ralph, I have a package for you, sir.' He reached under the desk and produced a faintly familiar looking box, and an envelope embossed with the hotel's crest.

'Thanks.' Who the hell was leaving him presents?

The mafia and the triads were all dead, and he'd come to New York alone.

Dodging the shouty firemen who were ordering people out into the snow, he slipped back into the gents and placed the Jimmy Choo shoebox on the sink. He stared at it. He'd seen it before but couldn't remember where. Maybe the contents of the envelope would shed some light?

The notepaper was, of course, hotel notepaper, so no clues there. The single line of copperplate script not only gave no insight as to who left the box, it presented a further mystery. It said simply *for my favourite actor* and was signed with a letter C. Who was C, and what was in the damned box? Considering his experiences of the past few hours, he was reluctant to find out, though. Having tangled with the highest echelons of organised crime, he wouldn't have been surprised to discover a severed foot nestling amongst the tissue. Curiosity, however, was a bitch. He didn't want to look, but he had to. He picked it up as gently as he could and put an ear to it. No ticking, but then again, this *was* the twenty first century. Bombs were detonated by mobile phones. He'd seen it done in plenty of movies. He placed it back on the sink. Shit or bust, he had to do it. He'd survived too much in the past few hours to just walk away.

Gripping the lid tightly in both fists, he took a deep breath. His hands were trembling and dampening fast. It was like an episode of that TV show *Deal or No Deal*, only with the risk of death instead of an empty box.

The ringing in his ears intensified, and his heartrate trebled. Was he going to die? He could just hand it over to the fire fighters and walk away. What if it was something seriously incriminating, though? He could end up with a life sentence for something he didn't do.

He'd overthought it, though. Hadn't he? Without another hesitation he ripped off the lid and dived under the sink.

There was no Richter-scale explosion, just the clatter of cardboard skittering across the restroom floor.

His heart was battering the insides of his ribs, and his legs were so wobbly, they could barely support him as he looked down into the box.

It was the vase from outside the conference suite. He'd been given a vase that belonged to the hotel. He shook his head. Why? Why did someone... His thought process did a sideways leap. The vase was old, and it had pictures of blue dragons on it. It also had Chinese writing on it. He'd seen the midas cat vaporise its twin.

'Oh shit,' he said to the, thankfully, empty room. He was holding a priceless artefact. He had to find out who'd left it for him and give it back.

The lobby was now empty apart from firemen and police. There were no guests and no concierge.

'Err, hi,' he said to the nearest fireman, hoping that he wouldn't ask about the box, or the fact that he looked like a famous gangster.

'You can't be in here,' was the only response he got. 'Get outta here.'

One of New York's finest took him by the shoulder. 'Didn't you hear the alarm?'

He was back out in the snow with a stolen Ming vase in a shoebox. If he got caught with it, he'd go to prison, so what was he going to do now?

CHAPTER 19

The Cat

The lobby was bouncing, and with Adam Ant's *Puss in Boots* playing on her iPod, it looked to Cat as though an intricately choreographed dance was taking place. She didn't have time for any of that, though; she had important business to attend to.

The old vase fitted snugly in the shoebox. It was perfect, in fact. The hotel notepaper, envelope and pen she'd borrowed from the concierge would top things off nicely, as well.

For my favourite actor, she wrote in her best paw-writing. Well, he *was* her favourite actor. The street theatre he'd starred in back in September was fantastic. He'd even done all his own stunts, and she'd never had the chance to thank him for his brilliant performance. Signing the note with a big C for Cat, she slid the note into the envelope and headed back to the concierge.

'Oh, hello,' she said.

The man wore a jacket and tie and had a nose of such length, Cat wouldn't have been surprised if he didn't need to alert air traffic control when he visited the airport.

'Uh?' He looked left and right. Everywhere other than down at Cat.

'Down here.' She seriously considered finishing the sentence with *dumb-arse*, but when you're trying to get someone to do something for you, it was best not to insult them.

'I need you to give this to someone for me.' She handed him the box and envelope. 'His name is Ralph, he's wearing a *You're Next* suit, he's bald, and he's got a glass eye.'

Before the concierge had a chance to reply, she stuffed in her earbuds and stepped out into the snowy night. A Broadway show would be the perfect antidote for cold back paws. *Cats* maybe?

The muffled boom that accompanied Adam Ant was sort of familiar. She was sure she'd heard it before. That was it. It was when she'd gone to the wrong hotel. Either these were updated tracks with explosive backing on them, or there was something badly wrong with her iPod. Whatever it was, she was too cold to waste time figuring it out. She needed transport, and an ideal solution had just rolled up. Two New York police cruisers had arrived, and the cops had piled out of them. There were four cops and two cars. Surely they wouldn't mind doing a car share?

Slipping into the one at the front, she adjusted the seat and pulled gently away from the kerb.

CHAPTER 20

Ralph

As the adrenaline drained out of Ralph's system, the cold hustled in, and he shivered so violently, he thought he might drop his precious cargo.

'Taxi!' He had no idea where he might go, but at least he'd be in a nice warm car.

Vincenzo was dead along with his entire gang. Xao was dead along with *his* entire gang, and as the cab inched through the snow-packed chaos, thoughts of what to do next circled his thawing mind. He had a priceless antique in a shoebox. No, that wasn't quite the full picture, though. He had a *stolen* priceless antique along with a note signed C. This entire shitscapade was down to the midas cat. It destroyed one of the vases, but it also exited the conference suite just before the explosion, making Vincenzo chase after it. That simple act had probably saved his life. If the fat bastard hadn't chased the cat in the first place, Ralph would have been in the room facing Xac's mob and would have either been executed or blown up. That brought him back to the vase and note. Could C stand for cat? Why the hell would it do such a thing? Whatever its reasoning, he didn't want anything to do with the damned vase. If he left it somewhere where the authorities could find it, it would probably get nicked, and he did look like Mickey Eyeball. Doing that would lead to his arrest. That only left one option.

'Take me to the nearest police station.'

'So let me see if I've got this straight.' The cop behind the desk put his doughnut back on the plate, licked his fingers and picked up a pen. 'Your name is Ralph Williams, and you've been mistaken for Mickey Eyeball. Not only that, but a secret admirer who thinks you're an actor managed to steal one of the Twin Mings from the mafia before giving it to you.' He looked up from his notepad. 'This ain't fucking April. If you don't leave by the time I count to five I'll...'

Ralph never got to find out what the cop would do, because as soon as he placed the Ming on the desk, the policeman's mouth stopped working.

Christmas Eve.

'Yeah, that's right. Yeah, the mafia *and* the triads.' As soon as his flight had landed at Heathrow, the reporters had pounced, and even the day before Christmas, the phone hadn't stopped ringing. Every paper from The Times to The Hampshire Gazette wanted to know details of how he'd single handedly destroyed two of New York's largest crime syndicates by infiltrating the cosa nostra.

Having spent his final night in the Big Apple being questioned relentlessly, it came as a massive relief when the CSIs confirmed the identity of the body found in The Harrington Building as that of Michael O' Donovan, AKA Micky Eyeball. If Mickey Eyeball was dead, then Ralph couldn't be him. That meant Ralph's story needed a positive spin, so here he was, a medalled-up hero with a pending book deal fielding press calls. As soon as he put the phone down, it rang again. 'Hello.' Ralph wondered who wanted an interview now. Your Cat magazine?

'Merry Christmas, Ralph.' The voice at the other end of the line almost stopped his heart. It was a voice he hadn't heard in a very long time.

'L-Lauren?' The only woman he had ever truly loved. The woman he'd failed to get a midas cat for. The woman he'd so gladly go through every hellish second again for, had phoned him up.

'Yes, Ralph.' She paused for less than a second, but it felt like hours. 'Would you like to meet for a coffee?'

Also by Tommy Ellis.

The Midas Cat: The Devil Wears Tabby. Available as eBook and paperback.
The Midas Cat 2: Rolph's Revenge. Available as eBook and paperback.
The Midas Cat: The Harrington Collection. Available as ebook and audio book.

Short horror stories by Tommy Ellis.

Fast Forward. Published by Horla Horror and The Night's End Podcast.
The Viewing. Published by Horla Horror.
The Book. Published by Horla Horror.
The Quantum Sax. Published by Horla Horror.

A small request.
If you have a minute to spare, please consider leaving a short review of this book. You input is appreciated.   Thank you.

www.ingramcontent.com/pod-product-compliance
Lightning Source LLC
Chambersburg PA
CBHW070653220526
45466CB00001B/415